THE JAMES NEW YEA

Volume 2

A selection of short stories of mystery, supernatural and suspense told at the New Year Eve's party hosted by Lord and Lady Grasceby of Grasceby Manor.

Based on the characters found in the James Hansone Ghost Mystery novels

By Paul Money

COPYRIGHT NOTICE

ACKNOWLEDGEMENTS

The author would like to acknowledge the support and help of his wife, Lorraine, in listening to the idea of the second volume of 'short tales' and giving both invaluable advice, encouragement and editing ideas as the various stories were developed.

He would also like to thank the following for their support and checking of the manuscript to ensure it was readable!

Gill Hart
Mary McIntyre
Julian Onions

CONTENTS

PROLOGUE

NEW YEAR'S EVE

Early evening

"Welcome, welcome! Do come in."

Lord Grasceby, or Neville to his friends, ushered James and Sally into the hallway. He took their coats and handed them to Marion, the Grasceby Manor housekeeper who normally preferred to keep to herself, but had been roped in to help with the New Years Eve celebration.

To be fair, his lord and ladyship had insisted that for her help she should stay and enjoy the evening with them once the buffet meal was over, and assured her that she wouldn't have to come up with a short story to entertain the gathered friends.

That suited Marion, as she didn't have family nearby to see in the New Year with; with the promise of a bonus for helping with the preparation, she was quite happy to be at the manor.

Neville smiled warmly at them. "I think you may well be the last as we did say 7pm for a 7 30pm start. Amelia, will you take our guests in to the others in the dining room and once Marion is back we can have our buffet before retiring to the study for the wondrous tales I'm sure we shall hear tonight."

Amelia smiled as she greeted James and Sally

and began to lead them along the hallway to the dining room. It was plain there was a lot of noise from the many guests assembled.

"Good to see you both and once again, Sally, many thanks for helping me out with my ghostly problem I'm glad we resolved our other little matter."

"So am I and it was quite an experience I can tell you. I am glad we sorted out our problem too and if I may, I'd like to pop up on occasions to continue our little chats, what do you say?"

"Excellent, yes indeed, nice to have 'girls talk' when Neville and James are not around."

They entered the dining room to much merriment as James looked about the room.

Phil and Glennis were present as was Joe. Harri sat next to him, having gone on ahead whilst James and Sally had dealt with an unusual phone call. Mark and his wife, Stephanie, were also sat chatting to each other but Charles and Fred were notable by their absence as was Andrea and Malcolm from the archaeological team. Marcus and Jenny completed the guest list and all were seated, smiling as James and Sally entered the room and took the places indicated to them by Amelia.

She smiled at them all. "Sorry to have to say that Charles is down with his sister this Christmas and Fred is not too well, so I'm sure we all hope he gets better soon. Andrea and Malcolm are staying with their boss, Peter for Christmas too so can't be with us this time. Otherwise we're all here now. Oh, Heather wanted to spend New Years Eve with her friends in Horncastle and we've been assured she won't get into any mischief, heaven forbid!

We did say we'd report her to Sally if she did bring our name into disrepute, I won't tell you what her reply was to that so, Sally, let's hope we don't need you tomorrow morning eh?"

Sally smiled as a few looked towards her. Neville entered with Marion shortly after, pushing a drinks trolley into the room. Sally glanced around at the assembled throng.

"Now, don't worry, I'm not going to spy on you even though I am now back on the force as a freelance consultant. But it does go without saying, don't drink anything if you are going to drive!"

"Hear, hear, I second that," remarked Neville. "That's why we have various soft drinks available too!"

Marion wandered round the large table sorting out the drinks as everyone idly chatted amongst themselves as the aroma of the evening's dinner wafted through making all assembled quite hungry. Marion joined them at the table once the various plates of cold meats and dishes of salad, pastries, sausage rolls, (home made of course), pies, dressings of all varieties were laid out for everyone to get stuck into.

It was scrumptious too!

#

Everyone around the table was feeling replete as Amelia stood up and tapped her spoon lightly against her wine glass.

"Well, everyone, hopefully you all enjoyed that. Marion and I have slaved over this today and it looks like we must have done a good job as there's little left! I hope we met and exceeded your expectations Marcus, I know how good the reputation is for the meals down at the inn, perhaps we've given you stiff competition tonight!"

"I'm going to have to watch out, I hope you don't plan on opening a restaurant with that 'De Grasceby' museum of yours! Any news on when it will open your lordship?"

"Oh come now Marcus, tonight we are all friends, so you can call me Neville. If all goes well, we may be able to open mid to late next year, so fingers crossed; no plans for a restaurant I can assure you! Anyway, time for the tales. Is there anyone who wishes to get us started?"

There were a few nervous chuckles but then Joe spoke up.

"If you all don't mind, perhaps I can start your lords-Neville."

"Be my guest. Oh, just be aware that it's now 9:35pm so we must be finished ten minutes before the New Year chimes in, so we can refresh our glasses for the New Years' toast.

Over to you, Joe."

Joe stood up and cleared his throat …

1: JOE'S OFFERING:
THE KNIGHTED TREE ...

"Firstly, many thanks for such a great and lavish meal, I think I'm now officially fat! When it comes to giving a short story or tale, I hope this is the sort of thing you were thinking of when you said a short mystery style story. To set the scene, I lived not too far from a small wood that bordered the site of a battle from the English civil war. I won't say where but this is what happened to a good friend and myself when I was much younger and I guess I was quite impressionable and I've never forgotten it.

It's never been explained and if I'm honest I sometimes think back and wonder if it was all a hallucination. I've changed the name of my friend to spare him in case by some weird circumstance any of you know him and he found out I was telling this story. He and I did get told off by our parents for telling porkies, so this is the first time in years that I feel I can tell it. And so I will begin the Tale of the Knighted Tree ...

Anyhow, a bit of information for you as we begin with Wenson Woods, an idyllic small patch of woodland on the outskirts of a hamlet in northern Lincolnshire. As boys we explored the many footpaths and animal tracks that led across the fields, through the woods and up into the Lincolnshire Wolds. It was our playground, something that sadly, city kids couldn't really appreciate or enjoy, even today.

It didn't bother Martin and I that we were trespassing on several farmers' land. No, to us, we were on adventures in our mind's eye and the open countryside was just that, open for us to play in and explore.

Sometimes in our wild imaginations, various distant landmarks were other planets and we battled space aliens and ships from across the galaxy as we travelled from one to the other.

Other times we were swashbuckling pirates sailing the seven seas in search of treasure and those landmarks were islands that could have treasure or be hiding a king's elite navy in one of their many coves. That was one of our favourites if I'm honest.

Sometimes we were world war one flying aces flying between battle scarred airfields somewhere over France, bear in mind we were just school kids and didn't pay much attention to history classes so at that time we didn't even know where France was!

I do remember that this particular time we were getting a bit beyond ourselves. We knew not to damage things but didn't know our parents had intervened when one farmer brought up the subject of us wandering across his fields when they met up at a local church event.

Our parents suspected we explored a large area and at the time we boys didn't know that they decided to talk to the various farmers about our exploits. It was agreed that as long as we didn't disturb the sheep, cattle and that when crops were just poking through the soil we didn't trample them down, then we could roam across the fields and valleys. It really was a different age from today where, unless you follow official footpaths, you can soon be chased off or even prosecuted for trespassing. Oh how times have changed.

Anyhow, one of the golden rules was that a main road lay three miles away and that we were forbidden to cross the road. We were told it was much too busy and dangerous and that was our limit, the furthest we could go in that direction. Well, you can imagine that if you get told not to do something, well, you tend to go ahead and do it don't you!

Well, I was always reticent to break that rule as I was the more timid of the two of us and I didn't want to get into trouble, but not Martin. Oh no, he was the fearless one!

He and I, this one day, had been explorers yet again, seeking out new lands and our latest adventure took us to that limit and, as we play acted closer and closer to the main road, I began to get nervous.

I stopped just as Martin looked towards the hedge, spotted the gate and mischievously gestured towards it hinting that he wanted to push the limit, go across and explore new lands.

On the other side of the road, no less!

We went up to the gate but it was clear the road was very busy. Nonetheless he looked yearningly at the other side of the road but I was too scared and told him so.

He was a little bullish and h..."

"Where's the knight then?" butted in Marcus as everyone looked round at him and gave him stern looks. "I'm getting there, just laying the foundations, so to speak. You don't read a book or watch a film and see the ending first now do you!"

Joe shook his head and continued ...

"Martin found it padlocked so climbed over the gate and started towards the road, looking back at me but I saw in a flash what was going to happen and I frantically shouted and gestured to him.

Just in time as he reached the grassy verge a large lorry sped by, just missing him as the driver honked his horn several times.

Talk about turning white. Martin ran back, jumped over the gate and stood shaking at his near miss.

"Told you, you daft sod!" I said more annoyed rather than angry at my friend. Also relieved as I didn't want to have to run back home and explain what had happened to him.

He stood taking in gulps of air then settled down and we both burst out laughing. Once settled he looked a bit further down the field we'd just come up and spotted over in the distance, Wenson Woods. Now to be honest, we'd sort of been put off by rumours of a voice in the woods that comes out of thin air. The locals all thought it was haunted, so most of the time we'd skirted round it to go up into the Wolds.

Martin looked towards it and pointed.

"Hey up, time to find out if it really is haunted!"

He didn't wait for me and set off with a quick pace, so I had no choice but to run and catch him up. He was a bit like that, impetuous! He called it being brave, I know what I thought but there are ladies present.

We approached the wood and, as it was autumn, most of the leaves had fallen so the ground was a carpet of rotting brown, orange, yellow and sort of off-green colours. Soft underfoot and a little squelchy in places as they rotted away ready for the worms to take advantage of them.

We entered the outskirts of the wood but we were a bit apprehensive as the sun was close to setting and so it was becoming darker with every passing minute. We really should have been heading back home as we didn't normally stay out that late but Martin was a hard one to say no to. I'm sure you all have or had friends just like that!"

Sally and James immediately looked over at Harri who scowled at them and several around the table chuckled. Joe smiled and then continued.

"We were about twenty feet or so into the wood when he froze.

"Did you hear that?" he said in a quivering voice.

"Nope, nothing, what was it?"

"A voice …"

Now I was getting nervous.

"What's it say?" I asked quietly, so as not to disturb whoever it was.

"E're lad, time to get theeself back home for tea yer rum 'un!"

Martin did a great impression of my mum and we fell about laughing.

"Hello?"

We stopped dead still and looked at each other.

"Hello?"

I could see that Martin's lips hadn't moved and it was clear he was thinking the same about me.

Who was calling out to us?

"Hello?"

We looked around expecting to see the farmer trying to scare us so we'd not come back, but there was no one in sight. Nothing but the trees of the wood whose branches were beginning to take on all sorts of shapes now we'd been spooked. You'd be surprised how much your imagination can take over and run riot!

"Martin, stop pissing me about."

"Its not me, 'onest!"

The voice called out again, *"Hello, come a bit closer so I can see you better ..."*

We looked frantically around but there was no one there. Martin did as he'd been told and stepped forward.

"A little more ..."

I was almost wetting myself by now I can tell you.

"Who are you? Why can't we see you?" I cried out.

"Come a bit closer and you might see me if the time is right."

"NO!" said Martin but we were both now rooted to the spot and strangely mesmerised by the voice.

"Please. It doesn't happen very often and I am so lonely in this state."

That piqued our interest. Martin stepped forward, one pace, two, then ...

"Stop. That is just right. Now can you see me?"

Martin's mouth was now wide open in awe and surprise and he frantically waved at me to join him. I did so, very nervously I can tell you, but still couldn't see anything except branches in the dusk light.

"Here, next to me." Martin pulled me closer and then pointed at the branches.

As he did so and I got closer to him, staring at the branches, I spotted him.

The knight in the tree.

Or rather, the branches had converged together to form a strange outline that resembled the shape of a knight in armour sitting on a horse. That's what I told myself later!

"Oh, there's two of you!" the voice said and it came from the tree knight.

"I'm Martin and this is Joe. Who, who are you and where are you?"

As we looked we could see a real knight on horseback with dull armour, but if you moved a little this way or that he vanished. It was like looking through a slit that hid the knight for most of the time, but if you lined up just right you could see him. A bit like seeing something out of the corner of your eye yet when you look straight at it, it vanishes.

"Sir Martin and Sir Joe, thank you for talking to me and not running away. I am Sir Stanley Goodweather, forever held prisoner by this infernal wood."

"Err, so you really are a knight?"

"Indeed good sir. But I am trapped, unable to move and can only look out on the world through a small gap."

"So, so where are you?"

"I do not know. It is a dark, bleak place and for some reason I don't need food nor drink, I can't foul myself, I can't move, I am stuck here for eternity. My horse is the same, I fear I am in limbo and I'm frightened as I must have upset the good Lord, our God."

"Oh, are there no others like you in there?" asked Martin, intrigued and probably like I, somewhat close to wetting himself.

"No, I am alone. I cannot turn, move away, move my body. I fear the Almighty has affixed me in place for some bad deed I have done, but I can't remember whatsoever it twas."

"How long have you been like this?"

"I, do not know. It feels like eternity. I have seen many wander past my view but most do not hear or see me. I do not know why. The attire they wear has changed - nay become quite odd, as are your garments, but I don't know for how long. There have been many seasons pass and I have lost count."

"What was the last year you can remember?"

I looked at Martin and nodded, it was a good question.

"The year of our Lord, 1415, November the twentieth. Very few have seen me here since then. What is your year?"

"1995," replied Martin.

The knight seemed to sadden.

"I am doomed to spend eternity here and for what reason? Why am I being tested thusly?"

"Err, don't know. Did you do something bad?"

"I was fighting for my King, King Henry IV."

I turned to Martin and whispered to him "He's a medieval knight, a real medieval knight!"

"Sir Stanley, we have a queen on the throne, Queen Elizabeth the Second."

Stunned silence from the knight. Then he spoke.

"Good lord! A woman on the throne of England? Nay, for the second time?" he sounded incredulous at the thought.

"She has been very good. The first one saved England from the Spanish Armada, or so my history teacher tells me in class. Our Queen has been on the throne since 1953," I said and saw that Martin wanted to burst out laughing at her majesty being on the toilet for so long. Sir Stanley seemed to sit up straighter.

"Then she has my undying loyalty!"

"So, you can't get out of there then?" wondered Martin.

"No, I do not know how to. I do not know how it

came to pass that I be trapped here. But I am gladdened that England still thrives. It grows darker out there with you, I am finding it harder to see you clearly."

"Yes, we need to be getting back to our homes otherwise our parents will be worried."

"Farewell then young sirs. Thank you for stopping and not running away like others have done. Thank you for talking to me. I am indebted to you both and hope we may speak again someday."

We were also struggling to see the knight as it was getting darker and to be fair we had lost track of the time. I heard a distant shout and realised it was my mother shouting at the top of her voice, wondering where we were and Martin nudged me before turning back one more time to the knight.

"Goodbye brave knight. We'll come back another time and hopefully talk again with you."

However by now the knight had faded from view and so we quickly ran back to our homes and unfortunately a good hiding from our Dads for staying out so late and making them worried. I went without any tea that evening and I gather so did Martin for making his parents so worried.

It didn't stop us going back.

We went back over several weeks but didn't see Sir Stanley Goodweather and thought that was it and we must have imagined the whole thing. Then in the spring we chanced on the knight once again.

"Oh, here he is, hello Sir Stanley Goodweather, we met you a few months ago, we're Joe and Martin. Do you remember us? I'm Joe and he's Martin," I said.

"Ahh, young knights, yes, I remember you well as it feels as if 'twere only yesterday. Months you say? I don't feel the passage of time like I used to when I was alive but I am thankful you come to visit me."

"So nothing has changed?"

"Nay my fine lad but your attire is more sombre, is it cold where you are?"

"Yes, they say it's going to snow in the next few days and quite bad too, so we thought we'd have one last try to see if we could find you again."

"And I thank you most sincerely for this kind thing you do for me, Sir Martin. Of which place are you from?"

"Er, we're both from Hammington."

Marcus leaned in to Jenny, "Never heard of it!"

All round everyone shushed him as Jenny folded her arms across her chest and glared at him.

Joe looked down at him and shook his head.

"Of course not, I've changed the name of our village!

Where was I? Oh, the knight seemed pleased.

"Ahh a fine place indeed. I am sure you represent it well for your King."

"Queen, she's Queen Elizabeth the Second, remember?"

"Oh, yes, and England thrives, I am pleased. Have you fought for this Queen?"

Martin chuckled, "Sir Goodweather, we are just boys out playing and exploring the countryside. We are too young for such things. We are also at peace, well, I think we are!"

"That is good to hear but lads that look your age have often been called upon to save our country from marauders, the French and Spanish."

"Oh, we're at peace with them now."

"Good Lord! We didn't cede any land to them did we?"

"Not as far as I remember, we are all friends now, including Germany."

"I do not know of that name for any country, I know of the germanic tribes so perhaps they united to form this place you speak of?"

I shrugged, history really wasn't our thing. "I guess so."

Martin noticed the light was beginning to fade. "Sir Goodweather, we will have to leave but when the weather is warmer and lighter we will come back and visit."

"I thank you and ask that you stay safe until we meet again."

We walked away but we never did see him again, we tried so many times, but nothing. Then we grew up and it just became a thing of the past and indeed Martin decided we'd been hallucinating and didn't want to discuss it again for fear of being mocked.

The end."

Joe bowed and everyone clapped.

"That was good but tell me, did this really happen?" asked Neville, a little scepticism in his voice.

"Yes, as best as I can remember."

"But have you been back now you are adults to see if he's still there?" asked Sally, intrigued but somewhat sceptical.

"Yes, Martin and I went back several times, even on the anniversaries of when we saw him but we never saw him again. As I said, Martin now says we hallucinated it all and it was dusk so it could be easy to be fooled and let our imaginations get away from us."

"Well, why not go back now and see what happens," wondered James, but Joe shook his head.

"Can't. The hamlet has grown out of all proportion and the wood was felled to make way for a new housing estate. There's a three bedroomed house on that site so I guess we'll never know."

Amelia clapped her hands to get everyone's attention.

"Thank you Joe, I loved that, so who's next then?"

Stephanie slowly put up her hand.

"The floor is yours then Stephanie."

So Stephanie began her tale ...

2: STEPHANIE'S STORY:

UNDER THE FLOORBOARD …

Stephanie cleared her throat.

"This was told to me by a friend who swears it really happened but I haven't been able to confirm or deny it. It's called 'under the floorboard'.

It goes like this:

As the little girl walked across her bedroom floor, one of the floorboards squeaked and she grimaced, her father had promised to do something to it but for now she guessed it wasn't important.

She called out to get her mother's attention.

"Mom? Mom? MOM!"

Her mother appeared at the bottom of the stairs and looked a little irritated at being summoned in such a way.

"Yes darling, there's no need to shout. Sometimes I can't reply to you straight away as I'm busy doing something that I can't just stop at the drop of a hat. You need to have a little patience, my dear."

"Yes Mom."

"Now, what was so urgent?"

"Have you got a small empty box I can have?"

Rachael sighed, having expected something a little more serious than a request for an empty box.

"Now what would you need that for?"

"We have made a time capsule at school and buried it in the grounds where they've started the foundations of the new sports pavilion. I want to do my own time capsule!"

"Well, that is a good idea. We did something like that when I was at primary school. Mind you they knocked it down for a development and I think the capsule was destroyed. Shame really. It was quite fun putting it together. Give me a bit of time so I can finish what I was doing then let me see what I can find for you."

Rachael took a deep breath, it was surely a coincidence after all these years? Lightning doesn't strike twice?

Does it?

#

Cheryl looked at the small box her mother had found after a long search.

"Best I can do my love, but it's a special box. Long forgotten to be honest as it had your first shoes in it. The shoes are gone but for some reason we'd put the box up in with a lot of your old things in the loft. Sort of keepsakes perhaps for if you have children of your own one day when you are all grown up."

"Thanks Mom, it's OK, just right. I can still put my letter in and something small."

Cheryl took the small box up to her room and pulled out her toy drawer to see what she could put in it. Her hand wandered above the items and seemed to be drawn to a few in particular.

"Ahh, the dog and cat figures from my farm set will be perfect, along with the Barbie doll," she muttered to no one but herself and put them to one side. She rummaged in another drawer for paper and a pencil but then thought about it and pondered for a few moments. Looking in her dresser drawers she found a biro so that her letter would last and be readable if sometime in the future someone were to discover her time capsule. She began writing, the words forming in her mind without her even thinking about it:

To whoever finds this box. These things are my favourite farm animal figures and doll and so they are important to me. I am Cheryl, I'm nine years old and if you find this then please add your own things and re-bury it.

Love
Cheryl XXXXXXX

She put the two figures, Barbie doll and the letter in the box and then wondered where she should put the box so it wouldn't be found for a long time. Getting up she headed for the door and the floorboard squeaked again. She'd heard it many times, and remembered her father, Frank, had promised he would fix it but had not done so.

Hmmm.

She was intrigued.

Cheryl looked down at the carpet where it touched the skirting board and knelt down, examining it. She could just push her fingers under the skirting board if she squashed the fluffy carpet down. The section at the edges of the room was still pristine and fluffy, unlike where she and her parents trod on it coming in and out of her bedroom. This bit was almost like new. Finding the end, she tugged and gleefully pulled up the carpet, then wondered if she would be able to get it back down so her parents didn't notice.

Rolling it up she uncovered the floorboard and could see a section about a foot long had, at some point, been cut deliberately but had not been nailed back down firmly. Using a toy knife and fork from her kitchen play set she succeeded in pulling it up.

Peering in she could just make out there was already a small box slotted in the hole and pushed under the remainder of the floorboard.

Excitedly she pulled it out and held it in her hands with wonder.

Nervously, she examined the box with its old tape and with her plastic knife, she cut the tape and carefully opened the box to reveal …

… a short letter, two wooden figurines, one a cat, one a dog and a small knitted doll. She sat on the floor and opened the letter and began to read:

'To whoever finds this box. These things are my favourite farm animal figures and my doll so they are important to me. I am Hannah, I'm nine years old and if you find this then please add your own things and re-bury it.

PS, my mother is a witch and has cast a spell on this

box, if you don't put your own box and this one back where you found it, you'll have bad things happen that get worse until you do as you are instructed.

Hannah. xxx'

Cheryl felt a cold feeling pass over her as if she were being watched. She hesitated but then added the 'PS' section to her own letter, sealed both boxes up and put them into the hole. Cheryl slotted the floorboard back in place then managed to roll the carpet back until she'd put the edges under the skirting board and, for all intents and purposes, it looked like it had never been disturbed.

Satisfied, she felt pleased she had found the other box, but a little disturbed at it having a spell on it. She knew she didn't have to worry as she'd done as she was told, but found it uncanny 'Hannah' had put the same things into her own box as had Cheryl.

#

A week went by. On the Wednesday of the next week her parents called her into the front room just before teatime.

"Cheryl, did you take up the floorboard in your room the other week?" asked Rachael. Cheryl didn't know what to say so kept quiet and looked down at the floor.

"Well young lady, answer your mother, did

you?" pressed Frank, firmly but as nice as he could.

"I, I wanted to hide my time capsule box. I didn't mean to cause any trouble."

"Oh sweetie, it was a good idea, but I started to notice the floorboard was squeaking more than usual so took up the carpet and found the floorboard loose. I don't know how you managed to lift it up as it was a tight fit. How did you cut the floorboard?"

"I didn't. It was already like that. There was already another box under there from someone called Hannah."

There was a pause from her parents as they exchanged odd glances then shook their heads.

"Oh, you mean this one?"

Her mother, Rachael, held it aloft. Cheryl looked on in horror. It was unopened and she was relieved to see her own box was still intact. Her parents didn't look cross but then she said the wrong thing.

"Hannah's was almost like my message, but it did say that bad things would happen if it and my box were not put under the floor boards intact."

"I don't like the sound of that!" Rachael looked perturbed.

"What did it say Cheryl?" Frank looked concerned now and a little annoyed.

"Er, Hannah's mom was a witch and had put a spell on it so that bad things would happen if it wasn't put back in the right place."

"I don't like that, it's poppycock. We'll put your box in but not the other, whoever heard of such nonsense!"

"BUT DAD!"

"Don't 'but dad' to me young lady. It's a load of superstitious nonsense and that's that."

He took Cheryl's box upstairs as Rachael stopped her from running after him.

"He's right my love. Nothing will happen to us, you'll see."

A short while later they could hear hammering from upstairs and after a fer minutes, Frank, came downstairs and popped his head round the door.

"There. You can't pull that floorboard up anymore and it won't squeak either now, so it's given me a good excuse to fix it once and for all."

Cheryl rushed upstairs but on not hearing the floorboard squeak, she walked back and forwards across it to no avail then flung herself on the bed and began to cry. Downstairs, Frank and Rachael had a brief argument before deciding to put the old box in the garage with the intention of burning it when it came to bonfire night, later in the year.

\#

Three days later …

Maths.

Cheryl hated it at school, and she was struggling with the examples the class had been given to work out. She did her best, but apart from anything really simple, she just couldn't get the answer right. Well, put another way, she often instinctively knew the right answer, but couldn't show any workings out and so was often marked down usually with a side note saying, 'You have to show how you arrived at the answer'. Who cared as long as she got it right!

OK, the teacher did!

A voice seemingly whispered in her ear, *"I told you so ..."*

There was a knock on the classroom door and the headmistress entered, going over to Mr Allister and saying something quietly in his left ear. He nodded and she left to wait outside the room as Mr Allister came over to Cheryl's desk.

"Cheryl. Pack away your things and go see the head. Nothing to be too concerned about, but she has some news for you and it is important, more important than this lesson my dear so make haste."

Cheryl did as she was told and on leaving the room there was the headmistress, Mrs Rawlingson standing waiting for her.

"Hello Cheryl, your father is here to collect you as your mother has had an accident at work and is in hospital."

Cheryl's eyes widened but Mrs Rawlingson gently held her hand. "It's alright, nothing serious but she's had a nasty fall so it's a precaution, that's all. Ahh here he is now."

Cheryl ran to her father with a terrified look on her face, but he just smiled at her as he picked her up and gave her a hug.

"She's alright. Just a precaution, but I wanted to take you to her now she's awake. It'll cheer her up seeing you, and me, of course!"

Rachael had fallen at work, broken her leg and banged her head, hence the extra few days staying in hospital. Over those few days, Frank knew Cheryl blamed him for the accident, despite not being anywhere near where Rachael worked. He wouldn't have it that he was at fault for not putting the old-time capsule box from Hannah back under the floorboard.

Cheryl sat on her bed, reading her book about a princess locked in a tower when she heard it.

A very quiet voice whispered to herself.

"I told you bad things would happen ..."

Cheryl sat bolt upright and looked around but there was nothing, no one but her.

"Bad things will happen until my box is put back. I don't have any control over it, but things will happen ..."

"Where are you?" Cheryl cried out just as Frank opened her door and looked at her, puzzled.

"Did you call me?"

"Er, no Dad, no, I was reading out loud, that's all and got carried away, sorry."

"OK. Good news, mum is coming home tomorrow so we'll be back together again as a family. I know you will miss my cooking!"

He closed the door and left as Cheryl smiled and thought that she much preferred her mum's cooking over her dad's. But he had tried to cook something nice and to cope whilst mum was in hospital and at least she'd had a few days off school as well.

"Are you still there?" she called out quietly but there was no answer. Cheryl opened up the book and carried on reading, perhaps she had dreamt the voice? Yes, that was it, she decided.

Rachael, came home to convalesce and life settled down to a more normal routine, albeit with Frank having to do everything, much to the amusement of Rachael. At least Rachael managed to show him how to cook, so meals became better and laughter returned to their home.

Cheryl tried several times to find out where Hannah's box was hidden. She sneaked into her father's study, their bedroom when both parents were downstairs, the kitchen, bathroom, living room and dining room, all to no avail. But there was one place she was not allowed to go into, the garage. It seemed logical the box had to be there so she carefully crept in behind her father when he was not looking and hid behind some large boxes and waited.

He went out. Now the garage could only be entered via the large remote-controlled door at the front as there was no other doorway and as soon as he reached it, he flicked the light switch and then his remote control and the door closed down. Cheryl had not thought it through and not knowing how the door worked or the light switch, she found herself plummeted into darkness and she froze.

"That was a silly thing to do, wasn't it?"

Cheryl stood stock still as she heard the return of the voice.

"Where are you? I was trying to find your box, Hannah!"

The voice laughed gently, *"Very good, I was your age, many years ago. One day they will tell you the truth. That's if nothing else bad happens. I don't do it you understand, it's the witch's curse you see."*

"I'm not listening to you, you're bad!"

"Enjoy the darkness then ..."

Three hours later, after screaming her head off, finally the door opened and Frank along with Rachael in a wheelchair rushed in and hugged her.

"I'm sorry, really sorry Dad, Mom."

"I thought I heard something but sweetie, this garage isn't for the car anymore, why do you think it's left outside? I like playing the drums, so it's been soundproofed so I don't disturb the neighbours!"

"This wouldn't have happened if you had put Hannah's box back with mine."

"CHERYL! Up to your room, that's not fair of you to talk like that to your father!"

Cheryl rushed up to her room and cried herself to sleep.

Naturally, once she became hungry, she sheepishly went downstairs and apologised to both of them and they gave her a hug and agreed to forget her outburst.

Two days later Frank was in the kitchen making lunch. He turned to plug the kettle in and as he touched the switch on the wall he flew across the room, shocked and decidedly shaken up. Rachael hobbled in on her crutches as Cheryl rushed downstairs to find out what the noise was.

He was OK, but puzzled. His hands were not wet at the time and he'd used the kettle thousands of time before. Rachael gingerly touched the switch quickly but there was nothing and it worked perfectly. Cheryl just put her hands on her hips and gave him a stare as if to say 'I told you so' but didn't say anything and knowing he was OK, she went into the front lounge and began to play, realising she missed her Barbie doll.

Then the voice whispered to her.

"I know what you are missing ..."

"Go away!"

"Your dolly. I had a knitted one, I put mine in the box. You had one that was not knitted, you put it in your box."

"Who are you really?"

"You know who I am, Hannah. I came before you."

"I don't understand."

"It's not for me to tell you. Your parents know. Ask them."

"No! Go away!"

"Very well, but that's two bad things to happen since my box wasn't put back. I can't stop anything else from happening, so if you want things to stop then break the curse and put my box back."

The voice faded away with the last words making Cheryl feel cold and frightened.

She went downstairs to find her mother doing careful exercises to help her legs get back to normal.

"Mom, I keep hearing Hannah and she keeps

telling me more bad things will happen, so please, put her box back under the floorboard."

Rachael looked at her daughter with a worried look about her. "Honey, you have to be imagining it, there is no Hannah, there's no one other than us in the house. Please, let go of this silly idea, for me?"

Cheryl looked at her feet and knew she was going to get nowhere.

"OK, sorry if I have upset you."

They hugged and Cheryl went back up to her room as Rachael sat down heavily, wincing at a slight pain in her legs, but more concerned at what was happening to her daughter.

Could it be happening again?

#

Two weeks later …

"Uncle Tim, Aunty Chrissy!" Cheryl loved them dearly and always looked forward to their occasional visits and this was no exception. It was her mother's fortieth birthday and so they had come for the day. Lunch came and went, presents were opened, and her mother was having a great day whilst Cheryl helped with the kitchen chores, washing up, tidying up and trying to keep out of mischief.

Late afternoon came and they all piled into the back kitchen diner to get ready for the main evening meal when all of a sudden there was a large crash and the building shook.

Just in time, Frank whisked up Cheryl in his arms and they all rushed out into the conservatory as the dividing wall between the lounge and kitchen disintegrated with a loud bang and the front of a lorry covered in glass, window frame remains and bricks, came to a stop just feet away from them.

From the shattered windscreen they could see the shocked look on the lorry drivers' face. He forced his door open and staggered out to join them, apologising profusely but unable to explain why the lorry had suddenly developed a mind of its own and veered off the road. It had been as if something had grabbed the steering wheel and he had been powerless to hold on to it.

Shocked, they just stared as they heard neighbours begin to call out to them and they piled out into the back garden brushing the brick dust and mortar off themselves as they heard sirens in the distance.

Uncle Tim and Aunt Chrissy's home was just twenty miles away and large enough for them to put Cheryl and her parents up whilst their house was checked over.

Without Cheryl being aware Tim and Chrissy knew of what had been going on over the last few months.

Tim looked at his brother and frowned. "So, that's three things happen since you defied the note in the box. Tim, I think it's time to take it a bit more seriously don't you?"

"Don't you start with this nonsense bro, just

coincidences, that's all. It happens to people all the time."

Chrissy looked at Frank and Rachael, astounded. "Seriously, THREE TIMES now and you still don't get it, do you?"

"Three times Frank, you can't keep ignoring it. My God man, we all could have been killed. We'd barely gone into the kitchen to eat when that lorry crashed through the living room and into the kitchen-diner. We're lucky to be alive. Even if you don't believe in the curse, then just put the bloody box back, what have you got to lose?"

"Frank, Rachael, we were almost killed! Next time you might not come out of it alive!"

"Think of Cheryl for God's sake, you have a daughter to protect!"

Although tensions were high whilst they stayed with Tim and Chrissy, nothing further was said and Cheryl didn't hear the voice. But she figured it was because she was not in her own room.

Incredibly, within six weeks the house had been repaired due to the generosity of their neighbours, local builders, utility suppliers and a crowdfunding campaign.

But with a great deal of reluctance, Frank now had a job to do.

He came out of the garage carrying Hannah's box whilst Rachael sat with Cheryl in the refurbished front room. With his claw hammer and a determined look on his face, he went into Cheryl's room and, after a few minutes of loud banging, he came back downstairs with a serious look.

"It's done. Hannah's box is now under your floorboard along with your box. Let's hope this is the end of it!"

#

Two more weeks.

Then a month.

Six months rolled by and they began to relax when nothing else happened to the famil. Cheryl sat in her room happily playing with her farm set. It was of course missing the dog and cat figures but she didn't mind and then she heard it ...

... a faint whisper called out to her.

"Thank you for putting my box back s ..."

Cheryl couldn't make out the last word, but she smiled and carried on playing.

Downstairs, her parents had opened an old photo album, looking with misty eyes at the little girl shown happily playing, as her father had photographed her.

Their first child, Hannah. Born nineteen years earlier and who had reached almost nine years old when she had been diagnosed with a brain tumour. Whilst she had time, she had persuaded Frank and Rachael to allow her to put a small box, a time capsule, under the floorboards of her room and they had honoured her request. Her mother helped her with the short note joking that she was a witch and that the note should be cursed. Hannah laughed at that and liked the idea and so without telling them, it was done and the box placed under the floorboard and her parents swore never to reopen it whilst they drew breath.

A short while later Cheryl was conceived, then born and as her parents allowed the memory of Hannah's loss to recede, but never forgotten, they enjoyed raising Cheryl. Little did they know that history would repeat itself.

When Cheryl came up with her own idea for a time capsule.

At the exact same age as Hannah ...

The end!" Stephanie exclaimed.

Everyone broke out into applause along with the usual questions of, was it real, did she know the parents and the like.

"Cheryl was my neighbour for a few years when I lived for a time in Sheffield before moving back to Lincolnshire. She and I were discussing strange things that happen and that night she told me all about it. So I have to assume it was real, at least to her. It's worth bearing in mind that unlike Hannah, Cheryl never developed a brain tumour and to this day is healthy and a happy mother too."

His lordship, mindful of the time held up his hands and everyone went quiet.

"Well, I must say this is all rather good so do partake of the drinks tray, bearing in mind of course if you are driving, not to drink. We all know who might report you I dare say," he winked at Sally, who just nodded and looked around the gathering pointing two fingers to her eyes then at them. They laughed as did Sally, but they all knew the awful death toll from drink driving and knew not to push their luck.

Drinks, and indeed, any leftover snacks Amelia and Marion had brought in on a separate trolley, were soon on plates and being munched upon as Neville again held up his hands.

"Well, who wants to tell their story?"

Harriet smiled sweetly at him and he beckoned to her to begin ...

3: HARRIET'S STORY:
The Toy Store

"So, my story is called 'The Toy Store' and was something I heard about when I was a sweet and innocent fourteen year old in my home town of Rapton-on-Dee. Naturally, I've changed its name for this story!" Harri paused as Sally was having a coughing fit as she put her glass of wine down and settled down with a grin on her face.

"Sorry, I was just taking a sip when you claimed to be sweet as a fourteen year old!"

A few laughed but quickly fell silent waiting for Harriet's reply.

"Cheeky! I'd say something else but we are in polite company so, before that rude interruption, where was I? Oh yes …

If we were bad, oh, sorry, I had several brothers so you can imagine they were a bit of a handful for my parents. So if we were bad then we'd often be told we'd be sent to the toy store. There we'd be turned into wooden figures and sold, never to return home. It generally worked too as I was, well to put it mildly, shit scared! Oh sorry your lady and lordship!"

Amelia just waved her hand, "No worries, I'm sure we've all heard far worse!"

Harri again continued, "OK, thanks. Well, I was good, you couldn't say the same for my brothers mind you, they were always right little tearaways, I can tell you. Drove our parents mad!

The toy store my parents were talking about was old and abandoned and no one wanted to buy it or do it up so it always looked quite spooky. It wasn't on the main street or market place but was down a side street off North Road, so it was a bit out of the way for the normal shopper. I'm talking about the late eighties by the way. For any of our ghostly friends hanging around in the shadows, that's the 1980s!

In its heyday in the 1880s to the late 1940s, you could find every conceivable toy a child could want. Often their own versions of many things heard on the radio, books and even from some of the movies of the times. In those days it wasn't as hard to make your own and sell them, nowadays you'd get sued!

They also made and sold all sorts of traditional toys and the sort of things you'd probably find in an antiques shop for childhood memories. Hobby horses, old toy soldiers, farm animals, multitudes of various makes of car going back through the ages and aircraft, to ships of sail and steam, you name it, they probably had it.

The store had been in the same family for at least six generations but destiny would make sure the most recent would be the last.

When it first became a toy shop, everything was handmade and the reputation of the quality of workmanship meant that not only locals enjoyed the toys, but their fame spread even to royalty of the time. Wooden dolls, toy soldiers, dolls' houses and the like were the regular creations of the toy makers. They were the Silverton family and in the early days being large families, most of the offspring worked in the toy shop at the back of the large three story high building. It originally stood on its own and was impressive with people coming from far and wide to buy, order or just simply gaze at the toys on display in the large front windows.

Their reputation grew but the family remained quite humble and refused to expand and build a factory, as they felt that wasn't in keeping with what they preferred to do.

Some say, that was their undoing as they could have become suppliers to the world as trade expanded and new markets opened up. But they were happy to keep it local. It is rumoured that Queen Vic even had a few of their teddy bears and dolls as a little girl, but that's never been confirmed. As the town grew, buildings and shops popped up all around them helping to keep them busy, then the two world wars came.

During both world wars they switched to providing uniforms for the men out fighting with only a modest number of toys being made. Once the second world war came to an end they went back to making what at the time were considered modern toys, tanks, ships, planes and the like for the boys and the traditional teddy bears, dolls and dolls houses for the girls.

The story was that what would be the last generation at the toy store always wanted to have children but for one reason or another, couldn't. So for most of their life, they decided to make sure the local children had plenty of useful and fun toys.

The husband, Mr Silverton, was very gifted and made lots of the toys himself, whilst Mrs Silverton could knit, sew and paint with almost any material you could imagine. So, he'd make the items such as dolls and she would clothe and paint them.

Just like in Pinocchio, they apparently longed for their creations to come to life. Hey, that's also like Frankenstein creating his monster, but I digress. Anyhow, they both became more and more eccentric as time wore on and fewer and fewer people went to the toy store. Times and toys were changing, in came spacecraft and spacemen, rocket ships, modern fighting planes and passenger jets. Cheaper imports began to flood in and it was as easy to go into the High Street and buy what you needed without traipsing up the back streets for somewhere hidden away like the toy store.

The other problem which I'm sure our resident DSI here would have soon dealt with, is the elderly couple seemed to want to keep any children visiting the store as long as they could, trying to entice them to stay with them. They did nothing technically illegal …" Harri glanced over to Sally who shook her head, so Harri carried on.

"Well, as far as we knew they didn't at the time. Now the following events happened around thirty or so years before I was born as the toy store was closed down when the couple died of old age, that would be sometime in the nineteen sixties. At least that's what we were all told in later years. But before they died, rumour had it that the couple had started to dabble in black magic in order to have children of their own to take over the toy store once they passed away. Of course, this never happened but something mysterious did happen shortly before their death.

Two children mysteriously vanished into thin air and were never seen again. Suspicion turned on the elderly couple, but a thorough search of the property found no trace of the children. With no modern DNA methods available to them the police concluded the couple were innocent and that the children who were childhood sweethearts ran away together.

But rumours persisted and not long afterwards some passersby thought they heard the cries of children calling out to them. The odd thing was it only happened to people who had adolescent or younger children with them. Single people or the elderly didn't hear a thing.

Ghost stories circulated, much to the deep upset of the parents of the missing children who refused to give up hope that their loved ones would return. It became old news once the elderly couple passed away in quick succession with the wife passing first then the husband, some say of a broken heart.

No one claimed the toy store, there were no apparent heirs and, as I mentioned, no one wanted anything to do with the toy store. Developers shied away from it, especially as it wasn't in a prime location.

Word had it that not long afterwards, around

the late 60's a homeless man sought shelter inside the building and for a time became trapped inside. It's unsure if he was drunk or on drugs, but when he got out all he could say in a garbled way was that the elderly couple had been working on a way of extending their lives and finding ways to entrap children and turn them into wooden figures.

He upset the parents of the missing two children by claiming they had already been enslaved to work for the ghosts of the deceased owners and if any child got too close to the store, they would be enticed in and turned into wooden figures to serve in the store for all eternity. They would be destined to become the children of the elderly couple forever.

No one took him seriously and he moved away. I did find out he passed away in a derelict cottage up in the Wolds not far from the Belmont transmitter, but I'm wandering from the story.

Not surprisingly, no one wanted to enter the store to look for the truth. It was the ravings of a mad, homeless man according to the locals. But to this day, some say they can hear the cries of the children and the laughter of the elderly couple as they converted them into wooden dolls forever to be their slaves and surrogate children.

As far as I am aware, the toy store still stands today in a decrepit state looking forlorn and lost. Ever since the homeless man's claims the two shops either side of it closed down with no one wanting to buy them due to the rumours. Two couples who started renting those shop's upper flats soon moved out claiming the toy store next door was haunted and that they couldn't stand the pitiful cries of children coming from within.

In the 1980s a TV programme was being made about the haunted toy store, but their footage was shown to be fake. However, in an unusual twist, unseen footage was released anonymously that seemed to show the ghostly old couple still going about their daily business in the store and two wooden children wandering the aisles as if searching for a way out.

So who knows what lies in store today if you go visiting the undead toy store in Rapton-on-Dee ..."

Harri stopped and bowed. Amelia clapped her hands and looked around for anyone with comments or questions. Naturally Sally held up her hand with a wry smile on her face.

"I've known you most of my life since university. How come you've never mentioned this strange toy store?"

"Trust you to ask, let's see, I don't tell you all of my secrets now do I? A girl has to keep something behind for a rainy day doesn't she!" Harri winked at Sally who shook her head. However, James took note of how detailed Harri's story was and mentally made a note to quiz Harri further. The look in her eyes hinted that some of it was true, and she was not letting them into something deeper. He turned to Sally and whispered in her ear. "We ought to find out the real place and go and investigate!"

"Seriously? She's making it up I tell you. I've

known her for a long time and she's never ever made not the slightest mention of this toy store."

Amelia gave them a quick look as if to say quieten down, then looked round the gathered friends. "Refills anyone?"

Marion quickly helped refill several of the guest's glasses then nodded towards Amelia who held up a hand for attention.

"Who wants to be next?"

Mark Hendriks tentatively put up his hand.

"Now, this isn't going to be like last year's offering that was all made up, eh Mark?" asked Sally mischievously.

"No, learned my lesson from last year. My story is from something that happened to me in the past, much like Harriet's story. I was around sixteen at the time and still living with my parents ..."

4: MARK'S STORY:
Footsteps in the night ...

"Some of you will know that I am interested in astronomy and space. I've been looking at the night sky for many, many years and had a sixty millimetre telescope when I was young. My parents lived on the outskirts of a small village, not too far from here as it happens, so I was spoiled with amazing dark clear skies. Not like today I might add with all the awful light pollution spoiling the night sky. Most people haven't seen the Milky Way because of it!

Sorry, it's my pet peeve!

Anyway I ended up lucky enough to be able to buy a second hand ten inch telescope from the proceeds of my bob-a-job errands such as going potato picking out on the fens with my mum.

Anyone else do that job? Blooming hard work. We stood on a moving trailer as the potatoes were wrenched out of the ground and, as they came up the conveyor belt, we had to quickly pick all the good ones off and put them in sacks next to us.

No? Good grief, you haven't lived if you didn't go potato picking in them days!

Anyhow, back to my story. I know, I wandered off didn't I, but I can't help it if I get all nostalgic. Now to be fair, the main cost of this 'ere telescope was paid for by my parents as they could see how much I was into the subject. They were impressed with me saving every last penny, so the next birthday they gave me a birthday card with more money than I'd ever seen up 'til then!

Anyhow, it was a sizable thing. They let me keep it in the conservatory and I would cart it all out bit by bit and set it up every time there was a clear night.

But I wasn't the strong strapping person in those days that I am now. James, stop sniggering! I found I couldn't keep carting it in out out and often lost time setting it up only to have the sky cloud over. That's the astronomer's bane you see, get set up then have to take it all down again in case it rains!

So Dad made a little concrete base for it and sorted a large tarpaulin and it stayed outside. All I had to do was unhook the tarp and wind up the clockwork drive and I could happily be out all night, that is before I went off to university.

Whilst in the sixth form I had plenty of lessons where I fell asleep, much to the disdain of my teachers. They did in the end raise it at one of the parent teachers meets, you know the sort, and I had to cut down on late nights when it was a week day. Weekends though were what I lived for, that is if the weather played ball and was clear.

After getting my 'A' levels, with distinction I may add, I ended up at Manchester university, did my studies on the newfangled computer age as it was just beginning.

Incidentally, that's where James and I first met up at Manchester university." Mark smiled in James' direction and he in turn raised his glass.

"However, back to when I was in sixth form I was still at my parents and, oh, I forgot, we lived next to the remains of the old village church and its churchyard. It was spooky I can tell you. I was always a little nervous when I was out at night, as you can guarantee there would be odd noises coming from the graveyard which was the other side of the thick privet hedge.

Now you have to understand, as I was a bit of a scientist, a nerd if you like, I didn't believe in ghosts or the supernatural. No offence to James, as we all get to change our minds don't we when evidence presents itself. Anyway, I once deliberately took my old 60mm telescope into the graveyard to banish the nerves, but only managed half an hour before I quickly picked it up and rushed back into our garden.

It was likely to be hedgehogs, badgers or even foxes as we had all of them nearby, but when you hear an odd noise late at night, your mind plays funny tricks on you, I can tell you!

I even managed to haul the ten inch scope into the nearby field as the graveyard had quite a few trees that obscured some of the sky. So - "

"Sorry to interrupt, but one minute you are talking in millimetres and the next in inches!" questioned Phil.

"Ahh, yes, you see when it is a refracting telescope, the one that has a lens at the front and you put your eyepiece into what we call a star diagonal at the other end, for some reason we always refer to the size of the lens in millimetres. With reflecting telescopes, such as my old ten inch, the mirror is normally measured in inches. I know it's a bit confusing but that's the way it is.

Anyhow, back to going into the field late at night. That was interesting as all I could hear was the faint babbling of the nearby spring and the occasional rustle of the tree tops as if a gust of wind blew across them.

It was quite an experience to be all alone in the middle of this field and I was in a slight dip which was nice and calm, but could get quite chilly if I remember it rightly. It was so good that I often got lost deep in thought, engrossed with viewing the depths of the night sky, thinking and exploring the cosmos. Luckily I didn't work in those days, I'd always have been getting into trouble for being late up!

I got my love of the stars from reading books such as the Observers book of Astronomy. Patrick Moore wrote it and many of the books I came to own as I was a big fan of his. Mind you the TV programme was always on so late at night, blooming annoying I can tell you. I got to meet the great man too, down in London at a convention. Amazing bloke and so dedicated. Anyhow, back to the field one particular night, late October it was, quite cool for the time of year but the stars, oh they were sparkling like diamonds on black velvet ..."

Mark suddenly looked at them all, lowering his voice.

"But then, I could hear it.

Sniffing.

Getting louder, not too loud but it was subtle and getting closer.

I looked around but only had my red light torch, we use that to help preserve our night vision, so you can imagine it wasn't very bright.

I was all alone, in the darkest depths of night.My eyes were by that time quite dark adapted, and there seemed to be small patches of zig-zag white streaks roughly heading in my direction from the small wood at the back of my parent's house.

I froze as they got closer and the sniffing got a little louder then suddenly the faint white patches stopped and the sniffing became very loud.

Then they began to move again and as my eyes were dark adapted, as they got closer, I realised what they were ..."

Everyone was sitting on the edge of their seats, all except James who had heard the story so many times he had to stifle a yawn so as not to spoil it for everyone.

"... three badgers! Two large, presumably male and female and one smaller one following behind them. What wind there was, was taking my scent away from their direction so they couldn't smell me, but they must have realised something was there, but they carried on, passed me and vanished into the night.

What with an owl hooting in the distance, the water babbling away and the badgers, it all added to the wonderful nature of that night and I'll not forget it."

Mark paused for breath ...

"Very good Mark we-" Neville began.

"Hang on, I haven't finished yet, just getting to the good bit! This was laying the groundwork you see for the next bit!

So despite all that effort and the amazing views of the night sky, with the Milky Way stretching high above me from horizon to horizon, I found it a bit too much trying to move that big scope into the field so I returned to staying set up in the garden.

Now my parents property had a long shared stoned driveway and our main grounds had a hedge bordering it with a few trees that had self seeded. My parents liked to keep them, they attracted the birds you see. They eventually spoiled the view as they grew taller and cut out a lot of the southern sky for me but by then I had moved on to university.

Anyway, one night I'm again enjoying the clear dark skies when suddenly there's the distant sound of footsteps that seemed to be coming from the stone and gravel drive that led up to the main road. They were way off in the distance, so I just thought I was imagining it and went back to looking at the Ring nebula, but all the while I began to notice the footsteps were getting louder and nearer.

Pad, pad, pad, step by step by step.

My eyes were again dark adapted, having been out that night for a good hour or two and it's quite amazing what you can see at night under such conditions. I glanced in the direction of the driveway beyond our grounds, but the hedge and fencing the farmer had erected some time in the past obscured my view, but I figured if it was a person then they should still be tall enough for me to see them even if just dimly by the light of the stars.

Nothing.

No one there.

Yet the footsteps were getting louder.

Now, there was a public footpath that came down the middle of our driveway but then went into the churchyard next door and a few years earlier we had been woken by our dogs barking in the night. It turned out to be some sort of scout group doing a night walk. By heck, Dad gave them quite a lecture, but technically they were not doing anything illegal but promised to be very quiet if they did the same thing again another time. As far as we know they were either very quiet after that or never returned!

Mind you they were walking through the churchyard so it does make me wonder if they were spooked by something in there. Perhaps one of them sat down for a quick rest, only to discover it was on a gravestone!

So the night I heard these footsteps getting louder made me wonder if it was the scout group back. I just ignored it thinking that at some point I'd see their dark silhouettes go into and pass through the graveyard. Better them than me!

But the footsteps got louder and nearer, so much

nearer to the point where the hairs on the back of my neck began to stiffen and I had a cold feeling inside me as there was no sign of anyone attached to the footsteps.

Now we had a three foot typical garden hedge that separated our driveway in our grounds from the lawn and flower beds, along with the spot where my telescope was sited. These footsteps seemed to come right into our grounds and I had had enough. I had a bright torch that I always used to initially get set up, so I grabbed it, turned it on, and leaned over to look up the garden driveway.

A bloody alsatian was caught in the light and was so startled it jumped up in the air and ran as fast as it could back up the driveway!

I instinctively yelped and jumped back because the hedge had kept the dog hidden right up until it was almost level with me. I'm not sure which was more scared, me or the dog, but I didn't see it again! I'm sure I too jumped just as high into the air with fright!

Later Dad found out that our labrador was on heat and even from a large distance apparently, the male alsatian was investigating and had come from the farm about half a mile away!

Bet it didn't expect to see me instead!

It didn't come back and I never heard any 'ghostly' footsteps again!

So there you have it, the footsteps in the night were not of a ghostly kind but sure did spook me!"

Glennis tentatively raised her hand, "So, it

wasn't a ghost then?"

Mark looked at her with a blank face as he thought he'd just made that clear.

"Er, no, it was a real dog, but the fencing up the long drive and the hedge in our main driveway hid it completely. All I heard was these footsteps getting closer and closer until it sounded like it was right next to me. That's when I shouted and put the white light torch on and looked over the hedge."

"Oh, sorry, silly me, I misheard you but it does sound quite spooky even so."

"Er, yes, at the time it was, I can tell you. Well, that's my bit done, I hope you all enjoyed it." Mark sat down as there was general all round clapping and agreement that everyone did indeed enjoy the story.

Marcus, who amazingly had managed to keep quite and not interrupt anyone for the last hour suddenly looked at Mark, confusion on his face.

"But surely, you could have told the difference between a dog's paws and someone's actual feet on the gravel?"

"Surprisingly not. As the alsatian was quite large, it made a good crunching sound on the gravel. Oh, yes, Dad and the neighbour had sorted a new batch of gravel and only done the driveway up to the main road a month or so earlier, so it was quite fresh and you could say noisy underfoot.

Bear in mind too that it was late at night, very quiet, and with a churchyard next door it doesn't take much for the ol' imagination to take over. To me it really did sound like someone walking down the driveway heading for our house. Happy now Marcus?"

"Yes, yes, sorry for doubting you!"

Neville now stood up and took over the MC duties from Amelia.

"I rather enjoyed that one Mark, many thanks. At least it was real compared with you and James trying to pull the wool over our eyes with last year's story. Mind you it was an interesting tale last year, nonetheless.

We're doing well with the time, who wishes to go next?"

James put up his hand as Sally groaned. "Don't you dare bring shame on us James Hansone!"

"Now what makes you think, oh yes, last year's of course.

So, shall I begin?"

"YES!" the rest cried and James stood up and launched into his story ...

5: JAMES' STORY:
Dig for your lives …

"This story is based on what could happen but as far as I am aware, it is just a story, so hopefully you'll enjoy it.

Let me begin …

Walking along the slightly uneven ground and down into the command station, he tentatively approached his commander.

He deferred to his superior who indicated for him to give his report.

"Sir, I have to report our water source has almost halved and we appear to have been abandoned."

"So, after all that has transpired, it seems we have been left on our own to decide our fate. The cowards whoever they are. So be it. The ground is still firm, what about the nutrient canal?"

"It still trickles but our best minds think it may not last more than a few rotations."

"What of the enclosure, have we found a way to break out from it yet?"

"No sir, it is impossible to break through."

"NOTHING IS IMPOSSIBLE! Let me think. We have no choice soldier, we must dig our way out of this infernal prison if it is the last thing we do. I see it is almost night, rest our soldiers then at first light let us begin to dig for our freedom."

"Yes sir!"

#

Once again the soldier entered the command bunker and his commander looked at him with questioning eyes.

"Report soldier, what news since we began our efforts?"

The soldier couldn't help but think that they were making the efforts and their leader was just sitting back letting them do all the work. However, it was not his place to argue with a superior, indeed, his leader.

"We are already down to a depth of three of us and spirits are high now we are doing something."

"Very good. How is the nutrient source?"

"It still trickles and we are on rations but our best minds now believe we can hold out for at least twelve rotations if we continue on our present rations, sir!"

"Excellent, we will persevere and succeed if our will is strong. Let them all know they are doing our peoples proud. It won't be long before we are free and can find our way back home to our Queen. Go now."

"By your grace sir."

#

They dug for nine days, slaving away as the sun rose, then rested at night. It did puzzle a few of the more intelligent amongst them that there appeared to be no sign of the moon and the stars and that they had been replaced in the firmament with diffuse glows and strange shapes.

However, they all had faith in their intrepid leader who had maintained tight discipline when they could all have lost hope, once they had been forcibly removed from their home and beloved queen. It had been a strange and terrifying experience, at first nothing too arduous and they had endured, but then they had strangely fallen into a deep sleep only to awaken to find themselves in a large enclosure with no obvious way out.

They again fell asleep only this time a few managed to stay awake.

It did them little good, for they described a crushing strain as if the world wished to engulf them. Out of fifty who somehow had remained awake, only two of them had survived, yet the majority of the original one thousand who had fallen into deep sleep were relatively unscathed. The two survivors tried to explain what they had witnessed but then succumbed to madness before they too died.

In the meantime it couldn't escape their notice that the sun and moon were no longer visible but had been replaced by bright orbs in the sky looking in on their, what could only be described now as a prison.

They had been abducted!

Who knows where they were but on checking

the roll call, they were around a tenth of the original colony's numbers, taking into account their tragic losses.

Their abductors had at least provided a strange funnel that had nutrients in which they could live on and a source of water, but otherwise, only a few small forest plants for them to live alongside. The ground beneath them seemed firm and was clearly of a type of soil but it didn't feel quite right. No one could work out what the problem was, but fortunately it didn't seem to be life threatening.

#

"Progress report?"

"Sir, the nutrient supply has failed as has the water. We have now lost forty eight of our number and it is becoming hotter."

"How deep?"

"We estimate twenty deep."

"And yet still no breakthrough. How is morale?"

The soldier hesitated, "Low, sir."

"I understand. I will speak with them when the strange suns have died down. Have them assemble for me and I will be there."

"Yes, sir."

The commander and soldier walked out, stood on the highest point and looked out over the assembled ranks, now showing signs of depletion, such was the way of the world and their seemingly impossible situation.

"Soldiers, workers, best minds. We are facing the ultimate test in endurance. It is now seventy five rotations as far as our best minds can ascertain, since we were abducted from our home and beloved Queen.

You have proven yourselves truly great in the face of such adversity, especially since the great disaster of ten rotations ago. We never asked to be in this situation, but we will endure anything that is sent our way, for we all know we will never give up. We will see our beloved home and Queen again in the near future, so we shall never give up hope, no matter what is sent against us.

I believe that no matter what, we will break out of our prison and march victoriously home and with your dedication and hard work I will report back to our Queen on how magnificently we strove to return to her, regardless of our losses.

Stay strong, dig harder and together we will break out. From now on, we shall work around the clock in order to break out of this prison and make our way victoriously home.

That is all. Back to the dig!"

"You heard our leader, back to digging for our lives!"

The soldier turned to see his leader walking back to the shade of his small underground abode and couldn't help but think that their illustrious leader was the one more likely to escape on the backs of everyone else.

But he kept such thoughts to himself.

#

"Sir, sir, I have grave news. The forest is dying and the air is becoming even hotter. I fear we are doomed."

"I see it soldier, but we must carry on. How many have we lost now?"

"Three hundred and nine, sir."

"That is tragic and we must not forget the sacrifice they have made for us. How long has it been?"

Twenty one rotations since disaster, sir. I fear we may only last for another rotation or two at most."

"That is negative thinking. I won't stand for it, I tell you. I need you to maintain your resolve at all times and remain positive for the troops. We will get through this. You don't want me to inform Her Majesty that you weakened and failed her, do you?"

The soldier looked down and apologised. "Forgive me sir, I have had a few weak moments when all seems lost. I will remain strong for our queen."

"Good. The air does grow stale but we must continue in the hope we shall break through into real earth and make our escape.

Proceed to victory!"

"Yes, my leader."

Suddenly a subordinate rushed down into the abode looking terrified.

"The sun, the sun, it is stuck a third above the horizon and no longer moves! The other orbs, they too are affixed in the heavens, we are surely doomed!"

Shocked, they all rushed up onto ground level and peered beyond the withering canopy of the forest. The false sun had indeed stopped it's relentless motion across the sky.

The workers and soldiers had climbed up to the edge of their excavated hole and stood shocked and terrified of what it could mean.

The leader looked at them not working and spoke. "Dig, dig for our lives depend on it. If the sun stays up then it will get too hot for us so dig, everyone, dig, dig for our lives."

He shocked the soldier and subordinate by running down and joining the many excavators. They all raced back into the hole and began digging as if there would be no tomorrow.

#

They dug, deeper and deeper, eighty deep after such toil, but they had no way of knowing how long they continued to dig for. Without the rotations to guide them, it could have been a couple of rotations or many of them. The leader perished, toiling away as if his life depend upon it. It had, but to no avail for him.

The soldier took up command, determined to see them escape, until a cry went up, a shocking desperate cry of failure. His new second in command raced up into the abode of the former leader, now occupied by the soldier, the new leader.

"Sir, sir, I bring awful news. We cannot dig any further, we have struck a layer of the same material that allows us to see the heavens above and we cannot break through. We appear to be surrounded by this material. There is no escape, we are doomed."

"Let me see for myself, soldier."

The leader proceeded to the base of the excavations and was shocked to see the dimly lit heavens gently shining through the clear base of the hole they had been digging. It had all been for nothing as the surviving workers and soldiers looked desperately at him for guidance.

He had none to give.

With no precious water and no nutrient channel, they awaited death now that it was inevitable ...

#

"Mission control, docking successful and we can confirm we are about to enter the station, over."

"Control here, go ahead Alan, systems appear to have stabilised and we read a normal breathable atmosphere inside awaits you, a little on the warm side but for now keep your helmet on until we can ascertain all is safe for you and your recovery team."

"Roger that. Opening hatch now ...

... Looking good so far, lights and power

appear to be nominal, checking control systems. Nominal, all appears to be functioning well within parameters.

No apparent radiation damage, looks like the old gal weathered the storm well. Glad we evacuated in time as I doubt we mere mortals would have survived the solar storm."

"Confirm that. Worst storm since the Carrington event back in 1859. We did the right thing evacuating you all a month ago, sorry we couldn't get you back up there any sooner but you know what it's like. Check out everything thoroughly then we'll make the call to launch team two in Star Liner 2."

"Roger that. Just coming up to the experiment racks, aww, our ant colony is, wow, will you look at that! Houston are you seeing this?"

"Roger, poor mites, looks like the artificial sun got stuck again without anyone there to keep checking it. Is that ... a hole in the base soil?"

"Confirm, looks like they tried to dig through to the other side, perhaps thinking they were digging a way out. I don't know how they did it but looks like they managed to use their formic acid to eat through the clear base and escape."

"Amazing, but a problem too."

"Concur, don't know how many got out as there are plenty of decomposing bodies lining the excavation site but being so small they could be anywhere and if they get into the electronics ..."

"We'll evaluate how to solve that problem but

for now we'll green-light Star Liner 2 and you check out the rest of the station. The Europeans are also launching later today to come and join you, so let's get what we can up and running and we'll deal with the ants once we have a plan. There can't be many of them left and without food and water they may well already be dead."

"Copy that Houston."

#

"Sir, despite the strange lack of weight our surviving tribe gives thanks to your courage and great leadership. We have secured this section of hard ground near to what appears to be sources of foodstuffs and water but there is no forest for us here. It is a bleak home but I believe we can survive after our ordeal."

"Very good soldier. We will continue our explorations when we have regained our strength and one day we will return home to our Queen. When we do, we will have glorious tales to tell of our exploits in this strange land of no weight. Having overcome this strangeness we are adapting well and the sacrifice of so many of our comrades of their acidic defence in order for us to escape, will be talked about for future generations in times to come."

"Long live the queen, and long live your courageous leadership."

The ants from the orbital experiment would not

be discovered for several weeks by which time their attempts at feeding on some of the materials in the space station had come to the humans attention.

However, instead of exterminating them, they were shown as examples of how a primitive species had overcome such severe adversity. The colony was eventually returned to earth to be studied in detail, especially with regards to how they acclimatised to normal gravity once back on terra firma.

The end," said James and bowed. Smiles all around as everyone clapped.

"Did that really happen?" asked Neville, looking astonished.

"Not as far as I know but I heard the short story a while back and liked it so much I read it to the point of remembering every detail."

Jenny looked at James a little puzzled. "You mentioned something about an event that happened in the past, Carrington?"

"Ahh, Mark can answer that better than me, over to you Mark."

"Oh, yes, thanks James. In 1859 two English astronomers, Richard Carrington and Richard Hodgson independently witnessed for the first time, a powerful solar flare on September 1st of that year. A geomagnetic storm hit the earth the next day and the aurora was spotted from all across the earth down to places such as Hawaii and even close to the equator.

If something like it happened today then, with

our dependence on electric gadgets, satellites and the suchlike, it could cause havoc! There's more to it, but it'd take up too much time to tell."

Amelia stood and got their attention, "Thank you Mark, sounds quite frightening put like that so I hope it won't happen in our lifetime! Right, still time for a few more before we have to get ready to celebrate the new year, so who's still got a story up their sleeve?"

Andrea waved but seemed hesitant.

"I have quite a short story so won't take long if that's alright?"

"Well, my dear, they are supposed to be short tales so do take the floor." Neville indicated for her to start and Andrea smiled as she stepped forward and turned to face her eager audience.

6: ANDREA'S SHORT TALE:
Snowy ...

"This is what my best friend told me about three years ago and involves her illuminated plastic snowman she brings out at Christmas time.

It was just the right size to sit on her bedroom window sill and when it became dark she'd switch on its internal little white and red lights. From the outside it looked pretty. When it came to bedtime, she'd always turned it off. Sarah and her partner, Gail, preferred the room to be dark at night when going to bed and they were lucky enough to have the nearby street light go off at midnight so it didn't keep them awake.

So this is how she told it to me, I hope you enjoy it.

Several years ago, Sarah's mother sadly passed away and with her father being deceased since she was a little girl, Sarah inherited everything, including the family house where she now lives with Gail.

It took her a good year to come to terms with having a clear out and deciding what to keep and what to give away or sell but, on clearing the attic, she came across the Christmas decorations. Now these decorations had not seen much use since her father's passing as her mother didn't feel that Christmasy spirit, so they stayed up in the loft. The only one that was put out on her mother's bedroom window sill was Snowy, the plastic snowman, as it was the last little Christmas gift her father had given to her mother before he passed so it had a lot of sentimental value for her.

Once Sarah and Gail fully moved into the old family home and they found the Christmas decorations, for their second Christmas together in the old family home, Sarah felt it was time to get them down and put them up.

Pride of place had to be Snowy and on the bedroom window sill he went.

A few days passed and one night Gail came awake, not sure why, but then spotted the reason. She gently nudged Sarah in the back who naturally awoke a little grumpily.

"Hey up, what gives?"

"You forgot to turn the snowman off."

"No I didn't I - oh!" Sarah had rolled over and the fairly thick curtains blocked most of the light, but still some light spilled up hitting the ceiling.

Sarah got out of bed and picked Snowy up, turned him over and sure enough the switch was in the 'on' position. She turned him off, put him back on the windowsill and returned to bed.

"Happy?"

"Yes love, sorry, but you were facing towards me so away from the curtains, and I was facing towards you and slowly came awake seeing the light. Night, night."

There was a sort of grumpy acknowledgement

from Sarah who settled down and together they drifted off to sleep.

Two nights later it happened again.

Sarah drifted up out of a deep sleep with nice dreams, very odd ones that made no sense but that happens doesn't it?

She was facing the window and curtains which were gently glowing away and she shook the sleepiness away and stared at the glow. "Snowy's on, Gail!"

There was no rustling from Gail's side of the bed and Sarah turned over. Gail was facing the other way, so no wonder she'd not been disturbed by the light.

Carefully Sarah slid out of her side of the bed and slowly pulled one of the curtains to one side. Sure enough, there he was, Snowy in all his resplendent glory, fully illuminated.

"I could have sworn I'd switched you off, come here you lump!" She picked it up, turned it over and slid the switch to the off position and all went dark as she felt on the window sill to put Snowy down. For a second she could have sworn someone said 'Nooo' but that was daft. Sarah looked over towards Gail who snored a little but was fast asleep, oblivious as to what was going on. 'She could sleep through a hurricane', thought Sarah but did smile that the slightest light usually woke her up. Not this time.

Then Sarah realised she had nothing on and she'd pulled aside the curtain, but with no light and no one outside going on a night shift, she relaxed, closed the curtain and slid back into bed drifting into a mixed sleep with dreams of large snowmen acting as streetlights as she and Gail walked down the undulating street they lived on. The rest of the night was uneventful

#

A few days and nights passed by with nothing untoward happening when Sarah again switched Snowy off before getting undressed and into bed with Gail, turning the light off only to spot the glow from the windowsill.

"Huh? I just saw you turn Snowy off!"

"It has to be a fault with the switch. I'll sort it now." Sarah turned the light on but grabbed her dressing gown so as not to shock the neighbours, not that anyone was likely to be up and staring at the house. At least she hoped not.

Yes, the switch was in the on position so she slid it to off and waited. It stayed off and she turned to Gail who was sat up, resting on one arm watching her.

"It did feel as if there was a bit of resistance so I guess I just have to be a bit firmer when I slide the switch."

Gail patted Sarah's side of the bed and once again they settled down for the night.

Until around three in the morning.

Snowy was back on. This time Gail got up and pulled the curtain aside but had a shock. Snowy was dark. She looked out and shook her head. It was a very foggy night and the fog was scattering the light from the nearby industrial estate into the sky, it was almost as bright as a full moon!

"Sorry Snowy, not your fault this time."

She went back to bed and nothing more occurred until close to New Years Eve.

No fog could explain it this time and Gail had watched Sarah carefully switch off the snowman just before they retired for the night, but there he was, glowing away merrily and lighting up the curtains.

"This is bloody driving me nuts. Right, that does it, batteries out this time."

Once again, for the briefest of moments she thought she heard someone faintly say '*nooo*' but she ignored it as a symptom of sleep depravation, at least that was how she was beginning to feel.

Sarah grabbed Snowy and went to take the batteries out, but then realised that it had a small screw that had to be undone before you could access the battery compartment. She stormed downstairs and was quickly back up with her small screwdriver and had the batteries out in no time. She put Snowy back in the window and closed the curtain.

"There! No more glowing for you from now on. We'll see if someone can take a look at it but otherwise, it'll be the bin for you! What did you say Gail?"

Gail was fast asleep and had not stirred at all. Sarah shook her head, climbed back into bed, switched the light out and tried to get some sleep.

Her eyelids began to droop and as they closed she began to have mixed up dreams featuring the plastic snowman laughing at her then calling to her not to throw him away as he swirled around in her subconscious.

Then she felt the world shaking and quickly surfaced from the dreams to find Gail rocking her, annoyed she had been woken up.

Sarah didn't need telling why as there was again a gentle glow to the room coming from the top part of the curtains, but she was now confused and concerned.

"I, I took the batteries out!"

Sure enough, Snowy was lit up and, as Sarah turned him over, the battery compartment cover came away and there were no batteries inside it.

It was impossible.

Then they both heard the faint voice.

"Please, leave my Snowy on, it helps me watch over you during the festive weeks."

Sarah's eyes were wide open as Gail held her by the hand and they embraced not knowing what to think.

"Mom? Mom? I, yes, OK, we'll leave Snowy turned on but once we take down the decorations, he'll go back up in the loft with them, OK?"

"Yes love, we love you both dearly and hope you have a lovely future together, love you. Happy Christmas and New Year to you both."

With tears rolling down their cheeks, Sarah and

Gail listened to see if there was anything else said, but it went quiet and they cuddled together under the gentle glow from Snowy.

After that, Snowy was good and stayed switched off when Sarah and Gail came to bed and they both kissed the plastic snowman before packing him away until the next year.

The end. I hope you enjoyed that!"

Everyone clapped and nodded in appreciation as Andrea sat down. Amelia looked about at her friends. "Still enough time for one or two more but after that we'll have to stop to see in the New Year. Who's next?

Jenny smiled and stood as Amelia indicated for her to begin.

7: JENNY'S OFFERING:
The flat cap ghost ...

"Hello everyone, it's been a great evening tonight so I hope my tale doesn't spoil it for you."

"You'll be alright my love, you'll knock 'em dead." called out Marcus as he gave her the thumbs up. The rest smiled and Amelia nodded to Jenny to continue.

"It seems many of our stories are based on when we were much younger, perhaps we were all more impressionable then, I don't know.

Anyway, I was about ten when oddly enough my family held a similar sort of night as tonight, the only difference was that it wasn't New Year's Eve or All Hallow's Eve. It was just an impromptu gathering of a few family and friends.

My parents let me stay up even though it was well past my bedtime as the adults were drinking whiskey and rum and began to tell tall tales and stories.

Ahh, I forgot to say this was up in Farrafoich, Sally and James know it well now, don't you, having visited a few times since sadly Mike Freshman died. Now, not to give a lady's age away, but it was a fair few years ago when I was ten, but I remember the night really well. Too well because of what happened later that night.

Now you could argue that I had been affected by the scary stories that a few had told that night and with just lamp lights on it really felt spooky to little old me.

Several stories were, as you can imagine, ghost stories with tales of ghostly bangings on the tiled roof of one person's house, the sound of a horse and carriage pulling up outside one family member's home only for there to be nothing out there but ghostly hoof prints in the mud.

So it was decided I should go to bed, probably around ten at night, this was in late November so it was pretty dark and the weather was awful too if I remember rightly.

I lay awake under the bed sheets and could vaguely hear them carrying on talking and I could also hear the wind howling outside. We had an old crofter's cottage that had been done up, well, done up for the times we lived in back then that is. So there was the odd draught or two and the curtains weren't exactly that thick, so there must have been a moon up as they were subtly glowing, gently lighting up the room.

I couldn't sleep, well, who's surprised at that considering what I'd heard that evening and I do remember burying myself under the bed sheets as far down as I could go, all curled up.

And then I felt it.

Something somehow urging me to peer out from under the sheets. I poked my head above them and froze with fear …

… two eyes were staring at me and I dived back under the sheets as fast as I could, breathing heavily and discovering I'd lost my voice and couldn't call out. I felt my throat was paralysed.

I peered out again and there they were still staring at me and I was transfixed. I couldn't move, couldn't shout for help, couldn't scream. They just stared at me, peering deep into my soul.

I managed to get back under the sheets in tears.

What were they?

Who did the eyes belong to?

Why were they haunting me?

I was shivering, not with cold, but sheer fright as I tried to think of what to do. But when you're only ten, all sorts of strange things rush through your mind, a bit like Mark mentioned when he was in that graveyard in his story.

After a while, I have no idea how long, I found enough courage to once again look out from under the sheets.

They were still there but not as bright as before and still the same size. They felt close and as if they were trying to look into my soul. Peer into my very depths.

I buried myself back under the sheets and shook as I felt so alone and terrified. Then help sounded as I heard footsteps coming up the stairs. I still couldn't get my voice to work, but then I realised the bedroom light had been turned on and I heard a voice:

"Sweetie, you all right under there?"

I slowly peered out from under the sheets and there was Mom, looking at me puzzled. The door was open and I began to relax. I must have been dreaming, having a nightmare after hearing all those ghosts stories.

"Sorry Mom, I was a bit scared when I came to bed but it's alright now."

"Aww, sweetie, we shouldn't have let you stay up but it's okay now, go to sleep and I'll see you in the morning. Night, night."

She gave me a quick peck on the cheek and I turned over facing away as she turned off the light and I settled down, knowing I was probably dreaming the eyes.

Then I felt it again.

A burning sensation as if someone or something was staring at me.

Slowly, I rolled over only to see the eyes looking at me again, piercing into my very depths and I began to breath in short gasps as I tried to call out for Mom to return.

"*MOM! MOM! MOM!*" I screamed and I heard footsteps come rushing up the stairs and the door was flung open.

Two things happened:

One: Mom was alarmed and asking what was the matter with me

and two: the eyes had vanished even though she hadn't turned on the light.

She flipped the switch and the light flooded the room as I shielded my eyes from the brightness until they adjusted.

Then, with no eyes to be seen I realised

something as my mother closed the bedroom door and went to sit on the edge of the bed, worried about me.

I could now see it.

My bloody dolly on the dressing table! It had glass eyes and as I explained to Mom what I had seen we realised the moonlight had illuminated them.

"Oh, I'm sorry love, I moved dolly whilst I was dusting yesterday afternoon and didn't realise I left her facing you like that. Oh it must have been such a fright. When I opened the door, the door was hiding the dresser so that's why you couldn't see the eyes when I was in here before.

Here, let me move her slightly so she doesn't look straight at you. There, is that better?"

"Yes Mom, the eyes point away from the window so shouldn't reflect any moonlight now. Oh am I glad! Sorry if I scared you!"

"Don't be silly love, I'd be scared too if I saw eyes looking at me. Anyhow, Uncle Eric and Aunty Dawn will be leaving soon, they're the last to go so we won't be long coming up to bed ourselves. Hopefully you'll get a better night's sleep now, eh?"

Mom kissed me on the forehead and I smiled at her as she turned the light out and I quickly looked over see if the eyes were still glowing. No, they'd gone now so Mom had done the right thing.

I fell asleep ..."

Jenny paused and once again Neville mistook it as her finishing.

"I have to say that had me going for a while, nice

one Jenny. Oh. Amelia, why are you looking at me like that?"

Amelia looked at him annoyed, "I think there is more to Jenny's story as she did call it the *Flat Cap Ghost*," she turned to Jenny, "so do please ignore my brainless husband and continue, I'm really enjoying this!"

Jenny smirked but avoided Neville's gaze as she launched back into her story.

"Naturally, after the dolly fiasco I turned over and this time fell asleep.

But not for long.

I felt something, like a presence as if someone was in the room, still watching me. At first I thought I was just remembering the dolly and that she'd been turned to face away from me.

I peered out and as my eyes were already accustomed to the dark, I could just make out Dolly was indeed placed side on so I couldn't see the eyes. I shrugged it off and turned over and tried to get to sleep.

But there it was again.

A nagging feeling that someone was watching me.

I poked my head above the bed sheets and began to look round the room. The curtains were still slightly aglow and as I scanned further to the left I could see the faint view of my shelves, a few pictures on the wall of Disney princesses and my dresser with its large mirror.

And that's when my heart went cold and I began

to shake, once again unable to say or shout out for Mom or Dad.

There, reflected in the mirror, was the dark outline of a man in a flat cap. I could hardly see any other features but somehow with that cap, I knew it had to be a man.

In my room.

In the dark.

Just staring at me, watching without a sound.

No movement, he just stood there, silently watching.

I dived back under the bed sheets, not that they would have protected me of course but when you're so young you don't think straight, do you?

I was shaking and I tried to call out but although my mouth opened, my throat was dry and only the faintest squeak came out. It would have been muffled anyway as I was still underneath the sheets.

I managed to find the courage to peek above the bed clothes and this time I looked towards where I thought the flat cap man was stood in the room and as I gazed round from the dresser mirror, there he was, standing silently just next to the curtains, staring, ... staring."

Everyone in the room was silent as Jenny looked around them, keeping up the tension.

"I again tried to open my mouth but just a rasping noise came out. What I did find odd was he didn't move at all, not even swaying or any sign of movement.

The Flat Cap Man was motionless and silent as suddenly I found my voice and screamed the place down as I dived back under the bed sheets.

I heard the sound of thudding on the stairs and both my parents burst into the room and turned the light on as I emerged from under the bed sheets.

"He, he, he was stood there ..." I managed to get out as I pointed. Mom and Dad looked at the curtains and there was nothing there.

No sign of a man in a flat cap ...

Dad flicked off the light switch plunging us into darkness and, as my eyes adjusted, I could still see Flat Cap Man next to the curtains.

"There! he's there!" I cried as Mom turned the light back on and shook her head.

"I'm sorry love, there's nothing there this time," she turned to my dad, "what about you?"

"No, nothing," he looked at me and tried to smile to settle me down, "sweetie, there's nothing there."

Mom bent over and kissed me on the forehead. "Love, you must have been dreaming, you know your uncle has a flat cap and they're stood outside waiting to leave. They were about to go when we heard you scream so they're waiting to make sure you are OK."

"That's a good point," Dad went to the window, pulled the curtain back and smiled, "Ahh, I see now, the outside light is on so it must have cast his shadow up to your window. That's what you saw."

I was now a little embarrassed and tried my best

to look as angelic as I could as they left the room, chuckling and the light went out.

As I became accustomed to the dark I couldn't see flat cap man anymore, so Uncle must have moved around the corner. I fell asleep safe in the knowledge that there was always an explanation and I slept soundly for the rest of the night."

Jenny paused and looked around at everyone and smiled mischievously.

Marcus led the clapping but James had a puzzled look about him.

"Great story Jenny, but one thing bothers me. I assume the outside light is below your window off to one side, perhaps on the corner of the building?"

"Yes, that's right."

"So its light would shine down on your uncle casting the shadow on the ground, not up to your window."

Jenny smiled at him as everyone started to think about that simple observation.

"I hadn't quite finished the story but wanted to see if anyone worked it out why it wasn't my uncle's shadow. Bravo James, I should have expected you of all people to work it out and you haven't let me down.

You see, a few weeks later, that had been on my mind as I spent a few late afternoons looking at the position of the outside light. I may not have been that technically minded as a ten year old, but I did like geometry and I couldn't make the angles fit. Even taking into account the moon, it was off to the right and wouldn't have cast his shadow either as it too was high up. Plus, the only other way to shine the light up was if there was a large puddle next to where he stood and so the light could have reflected off that and up onto my window. Except it hadn't been raining, just a howling gale, so Uncle Eric wasn't to blame.

Then a few nights later when the moon rose late in the night, I got the same feeling that I was being watched and this time I was determined to be brave and not let it scare me.

I looked across from over the bed sheets and there he was again, just a dark silhouette to the right side of the curtains but this time I didn't scream, I talked to him.

"Hello? Are you a ghost?"

Silence, but I thought I saw a brief flicker of movement as if he was caught by surprise by my voice.

"I'm not afraid you know. I don't mind if you are a ghost, but I do want to know why you are watching me?"

Suddenly he faded from view and the feeling left me, he'd gone. Perhaps I'd scared him away, I didn't know.

But three nights later the moon was full and lit up my room like the first time and he was back.

I sat up in bed and looked at him. I wasn't sure if I could see any features but for some reason I was beginning to feel sorry for him.

"Did you used to live here?" I asked.

A pause then:

"Yes, until just after you were born," came the reply in a soft, quiet spoken voice.

I have to admit, I wasn't really expecting a reply, it was more for me to stay strong and keep talking in case my fear returned.

"That was more than ten years ago. I'm ten now."

"Yes, your parents have done good by the place. It was a semi detached and I lived here on this side for forty or more years."

"That's nice, what happened to you?"

"I was old, passed away in my sleep. My housekeeper found me and was very upset. She lived in the other room but knew my time was near. This room used to be my old room. The stairs came up on that side.

I don't know why I keep coming back but I keep watch over you and make sure nothing happens to you."

"So you are my guardian angel?"

"I suppose so. I don't know how long for."

A thought occurred to me, "Are you watching me when I get undressed at night and dressed in the morning."

"Good lord no! I was brought up good and proper. I don't seem to be here in the daytime and only find myself here when you appear to fall asleep."

"Good, otherwise I'd be very upset. I'm going to sleep now, oh, what's your name?"

"Willoughton, Gareth Willoughton."

"Goodnight Mr Willoughton."

"Goodnight little one, sleep well."

I settled down and fell asleep. I only saw him a few times after that, but one day I asked my mom, who lived in our house before we did. She was a little surprised as we were sitting at the dinner table whilst I had my orange drink.

"Oh, there was a man and his housekeeper, a Mr Willoughton and Daisy, we often called him 'Pop' Willoughton. We'd only been moved in about eight months and you were on the way when Daisy found he'd passed away in his sleep.

She stayed in his part of the cottage as he'd left it to her, but then she decided to move away and live with her older sister so she could look after her, that would be about two years after he passed away.

Daisy passed away a year later, some say it was from a broken heart as we had often wondered if anything was going on between her and Mr Willoughton when he was alive." Mom looked inquisitively at me.

"Why do you ask?"

"Oh nothing. You know he was called Gareth and used to wear a flat cap didn't you?"

"How did you ..?"

"I did some research at school with help from my teacher."

"Oh, that's clever. Mr Willoughton seemed a nice person, shame we didn't know him for longer. Still, once Daisy moved out we were able to put in an offer to buy the cottage and turn it into this home."

My curiosity was satiated, I'd found the

explanation. We didn't talk much about him after that and I only saw him a few more times. He rarely spoke after our first time. Mom did ask when I was an adult if I had seen him and I was honest with her and we had a good chat about 'Pop' Willoughton.

It seems they too had seen him occasionally and that night shook them a bit as they knew he must have been what I saw standing next to the curtains. Dad had told Mom that the outside light couldn't have shone upwards like that casting Uncle Eric's shadow. As the ghost didn't seem to be harmful, they decided just to leave things alone and see if I said anything else. The last time I saw him was when I was fifteen and he said he was going away, he felt he was being called somewhere so I always liked to think he really was my guardian angel whilst I was young.

So, there you are my tale of the Flat Cap Man."

Everyone applauded as Neville checked the time, "That was very good, you can come again Jenny if you have any more stories like that. Anyhow, I think we have time for one more as long as it is not too long?"

Phil put his hand up and Neville nodded for him to begin ...

8: PHIL'S STORY...
The Eerie Nowhere Cottage

"Well, how shall I begin?"

'At the beginning" chortled Marcus. Everyone looked at him and shook their heads as he seemed to be more of a nuisance this year, which was unlike his normal self.

"Well, yes, so I guess a bit of background first. I reckon you are right Jenny, as when I was about eleven, I had a great friend who I got up to all sorts of minor mischief with, as you can imagine. We lived up in Waddington. No, no, before you ask, this is the one now in Lancashire, but when I was a boy it was in the west riding of Yorkshire. Bloody boundary changes. It didn't go down well I can tell you!

Anyhow, a bit like Joe and his friend in his tale, Tim and I roamed far and wide across the fields and dales and many a time we passed by a run down and quite shabby looking old cottage, which scared the willy wobbles out of us both as it looked so spooky. We'd often tried to get each other to go in but neither of us had the bottle.

Then one day everything changed ...

\#

"Go on, I dare ya!" Tim pushed me in the side as we stood outside the cottage looking nervously at the front door.

"No, don't want to."

"Scaredy-cat, scaredy-cat, who's a scaredy-cat!"

"You go in then!"

Tim hesitated and looked at the door in dread. "Shit!"

"Ha ha, ha ha, you said a naughty word. That means you have to go in now!" I looked triumphantly at my friend as we had always said if either of us swore then the culprit had to make amends by doing something they hated.

Tim slowly walked up to the door as I looked on in amazement. I seriously didn't think he would do it.

"Noooo. You gonna do it? Really?"

Tim looked at me with a nervous smile. "Yeah!" he lifted the door latch and for a brief moment he thought he had been let off as it was rusted tight shut.

Then it gave way allowing him to pull it and the door creaked open.

He hesitated as I looked up the valley.

"Go on, get in, there's a woman with a dog up there an' I don't want her to see us go in!"

Tim shook his head and stepped inside quickly followed by me, pushing him from behind. I quickly pulled the door closed and we let our eyes slowly adjust to the gloom inside. The downstairs front window was boarded up so very little light filtered in. Tim coughed at the dust we'd kicked up on the old, dull, red tiled floor.

There was a door across the room on the right and further along towards the front of the room was another door. I wandered over to it and pulled it open.

Stairs. Wooden stairs with a tight turn starting at the base before becoming steep as they disappeared out of sight. They didn't look safe, so I closed the door and shook my head.

"No way that I'm trusting them!"

Tim was at the back of the room, about to open the other door and turned to say something but instead just stared at the front door with his mouth open.

I looked at him, puzzled and as our eyes were becoming accustomed to the gloom I saw with horror what had spooked Tim.

There was no front door!

"Where...where...where's the door gone?" I stuttered.

The plastered wall stretched all across the front with no sign a door had ever existed.

We looked at each other in horror just as a faint voice whispered to us from out of the gloom ...

"Who will it be?"

Eyes wide open, Tim looked at me, genuinely scared.

"Stop it!"

"Wasn't me!"

We looked around but all was quiet. Tim turned and pulled at the door handle for the second room and the door opened as we peered in. It looked like a very old-fashioned kitchen with what looked like a mangle with a very worn wooden handle in one corner. Together Tim and I stepped through and were relieved there was no voice to greet us. We assumed we were imagining it, at least that's what we hoped! A back window above the sink was boarded up but one of the boards had slipped allowing a little light to filter in to break up the gloom.

A back door offered us hope and we opened it eagerly, only to be disappointed to find it led to a small privy tacked on the back of the cottage. Its wooden seat was rotting away and there was a space underneath for what I assumed had to have been a bucket. Clearly the cottage had been empty for a very long time and had never had modern things such as electricity or running water, let alone a sewage service.

A whisper came from behind us ...

"Who will it be?"

We spun round but again, there was no one there.

Tim was shaking now. "Phil, I'm scared."

"Yeah, me too. Let's try upstairs, perhaps we can get out from an upstairs window?"

I opened the door to the front room not realising neither of us had closed it. Stepping through, I stopped, surprised and shocked. Turning back, the door was closed and I could just hear Tim calling out to me, asking where I'd gone. He sounded distant and what's more, somewhere below me!

I looked at the room I was in. An old bed, with a mattress that was covered in bird poo with holes that I guessed must have been made by rats, that lay pushed up against a bare brick wall. I was somehow upstairs but I hadn't gone up the old staircase! Tim's frightened voice wafted up to me. "Where are you?"

"Er, I'm upstairs, I think in the front room!"

"How the…"

"Where are you?"

"In the privy!"

"What? Going?"

"No you idiot, but at this rate I reckon I'll wet meself!"

The voice again wafted into my ears, *"Which one will it be?"* whispered the cottage, startling me."

Phil stood smiling at his audience who were caught up in the mystery and paying close attention, some leaning forward as if that would help them work out where he was going. He knew he had their rapt attention and continued …

"Tim opened the privy door only to find himself stepping into the upstairs back room which had a small single bed with no mattress and the springs rusting away.

Meanwhile, I opened the door to the stairs and was relieved to see them in the gloom, even if they looked dangerous. I tentatively stepped on the first one half expecting to appear in another room, but the step creaked and took my weight. Slowly, ever so slowly I made my way down but felt the last but one step give way, so jumped the last couple of steps pushing at the door and it swung open as I fell through …

… into the front upstairs room again!

"Tim, where are you?"

"Back bedroom, what about you?"

"Front bedroom, even though I walked down the stairs, I'll come through to you." I ran over to the door and I could hear Tim doing the same as he opened the door, only to find himself back in the downstairs front room instead. I heard Tim call out in despair. "That's not fair, I'm downstairs now! What about you?"

"Front upstairs bedroom again! Hang on, I can hear a dog barking. It must be with that woman we saw in the distance. I'll call for help."

I ran over to the window which had no glass but wasn't boarded up. I could see the lady with her pomeranian yapping loudly as they walked past the cottage.

"Help! Lady, over here! We can't get out, please help us!"

She carried on walking, apparently not hearing me. She did glance at the cottage, but I reckoned from her viewpoint, the front windows were all boarded up, including the upstairs room. I cried out several times and it seemed only the dog could hear me, but it just barked then pulled on its lead urging the lady onwards. She carried on walking away, much to my dismay and shock.

The cottage spoke quietly once more, *"So, who*

will it be? A difficult choice but I've nearly decided ..."

"Tim, try the door again, we've got to get out!" I shouted then heard Tim shout something before going silent.

Tim had stepped up to the door but couldn't open it and stepped back terrified, then leant against the plastered wall separating the upstairs rooms. Quick as a flash he was pulled into and absorbed by the wall as his screams were cut short.

I was terrified and again I heard the cottage speak in a more menacing tone.

"One is enough ... for now ... But you may find a way out. There are three ..."

"Wha...What? Three what? Who are you? Where are you? What have you done to my friend?"

I frantically looked round, then something made me look up.

A loft hatch.

Looking around I spotted a large crate that I would swear had not been there earlier. Undeterred I dragged it over and stood on it, just reaching the hatch. It pushed up and the hatch flipped up and out of the way. Hope building, I jumped, grabbed the hatch frame and hauled myself up into the loft which was surprisingly bright. Part of the roof had caved in at the back and I desperately clambered up the rubble and hauled myself out onto the roof.

Spotting a slanted tiled roof further down, I realised it was the roof of the privy and managed to slide down it and jump down onto the rough, overgrown grass. I rushed round to the front of the cottage then circled it, but there was no door.

"Tim! TIM!"

"He can't hear you. He is mine now."

With that, the cottage faded from view leaving no trace as I stood, horrified and in shock as I began to cry for my lost friend.

I rushed back home in a state and tried to explain to my parents, but to no avail. Arguing with my father, I ran out and raced back to where the cottage lay with Father in hot pursuit, catching up with me just as we reached the site.

No cottage, no sign of old foundations, nothing.

"Son, I've lived in Waddington all my life and when I was your age and even younger, I too roamed the hills and valleys. But I can tell you there has never been a cottage here. Never."

"But, but Tim's in there and can't get out. It was talking to us!"

"Philip, Tim will be at home and I'm sure he's playing a prank on you. Now enough of this nonsense, come on, home with you."

I looked about and wiped my tears away with my sleeve, but kept shaking my head. Reluctantly I started to follow Father home, but then heard the whisper ...

"Until next time ..."

#

Next day there was a knock on our front door. The police officer standing with Tim's parents, introduced himself and asked to come in, explaining that Timothy had been missing since the previous afternoon. The last thing his parents remembered was that he was meeting up with me.

I was about to launch into my story of the cottage but I see the look from my father and I only said we were out exploring all afternoon then separated to come home and I'd not seen Tim since.

Over the next week I was asked to retrace my steps with Tim and every time I stopped at the site of where the cottage had been. I had to say that was where we went our separate ways.

I mentioned the lady and her dog, but the police found no incriminating evidence and couldn't trace the woman with her pomeranian, so the case went cold.

Poor Timmy has been devoured by the eerie ghostly cottage and was never seen again.

The eerie nowhere cottage had claimed its victim.

The end!"

Everyone applauded Phil's story and he took a bow.

Amelia stood and had to ask: "Is that a real story Phil and was it you or all made up?"

"Oh, of course not, all made up, in fact I was inspired by Charles' story last year about the hungry bark and the oak tree, so I thought I'd come up with something similar, but different enough, I hope for you all to enjoy."

Neville smiled and noted the time. "Well everyone, I think that works out just right so do take a glass of whatever you fancy and we'll see in the new year."

Everyone agreed that they'd had a good time and so another year was seen in.

Much merriment later, everyone shuffled into the hallway and collected their coats, thanking their hosts as they left, with the question of who would host the next year's event finally answered. Marcus would host it at the Star and Crescent Moon Inn.

The question many left unsaid was, would Jenny be with him or not in a year's time?

You'll have to wait a year to find out dear reader ...

EPILOGUE

As James and Sally had walked up to Grasceby Manor, Harri gave them a lift back home as she had made the point of not drinking. Slightly tipsy, James and Sally were grateful as it was bitterly cold out with a hint of snow in the wind.

But Sally was still puzzled.

"Seriously," she said as she turned the key in the door and opened it for them to be greeted by Scruff, "You have never ever mentioned anything about a toy store before in all the years I've known you."

"Oh Sally, give it a rest!" suggested James who immediately regretted saying anything.

"Oi! Don't tell me to give it a rest! You haven't known *trouble* here as long as I have and something is off, I can tell you know!"

Scruff was jumping up and down trying to impress on them he really needed to go out so James grabbed his lead and attached it to the scottie. "Sorry love. Look, I'll take Scruff for a very quick walk, yes Scruff, it'll be a quick walk this time considering the weather. You two go in and make hot chocolates all round and I'm sure Harri will give up her secrets, won't you Harri?" James gave her a look as much to say, *spill, you know Sally won't let it go!*

Harri sighed as she and Sally began to take off their coats as Scruff pulled at his lead and he and James vanished off into the night, or rather a quick trot over to the garage to the 'short stop' section

James had made for such eventualities!

Five minutes later they heard them come back inside as James towelled Scruff down who was soaking wet, not to mention James, then the scottie happily wandered over to his basket, turned around three times and plopped down on it to go to sleep.

James dried his head as best he could after taking his own coat off and joined Harri and Sally in the kitchen-diner where at least the atmosphere had warmed up between them.

Sally pointed to his mug of hot chocolate and smiled at him with a smug expression on her face.

Harri has a confession to make, haven't you Harri?"

She grimaced as James took his seat at the table. Harri took a deep breath and began her story.

"You see, it's like this ..."

#

Phil and Glennis arrived back home and she headed off to the bedroom. Phil, however, headed into his back room, his office, otherwise known as his den, and walked over to his filing cabinet. Fishing out his set of keys he bent down and opened the second to last drawer and fished out a thick folder, took it to his desk and opened the folder up as he sat down, heavy hearted.

He spent ten minutes leafing through all the cuttings he'd collected over the years.

Missing boy presumed runaway.

Parents cleared of any wrong doing.
Mystery cottage, a childish story without merit
Girl vanishing 'not connected to previous cases.
Mystery sightings of a ghostly cottage not helping matters and is hogwash says leading detective.

The cuttings went on and Phil shed a tear for his long lost best friend …

NEWSLETTER

If you want to know more about the James Hansone Ghost Mysteries or the other novels from Astrospace Fiction, such as how to purchase them and where, or when the next book in the series will be released, then simply sign up and you'll be the first to informed. There will also be a possible competition or a give-away so worth subscribing to see what may be on offer soon. Note your information will not be passed on to third parties.

Just head on over to the following link where you can enter your email to be added to the newsletter list.

Note I will not share your email with anybody, and it is only for keeping up to date with Astrospace Fiction books.

https://mailchi.mp/1c69765ddf7a/jameshansonegm-signup
Best wishes and see you soon: Paul

THE JAMES HANSONE GHOST MYSTERIES

It all started with a simple unplanned diversion, 'A Ghostly Diversion'.

James Hansone is a computer and IT specialist and a complete sceptic when it came to all things paranormal. Until *that* diversion. It changes everything once he becomes intrigued with a ghostly face at a broken window of a rundown cottage, deep in the Lincolnshire countryside. Little did he know that he would go on to uncover the mystery of a missing girl that would change his life forever.

Now with six sequels, James Hansone unwittingly becomes a ghost hunter roped in to explore further mysteries with more books planned in the series.

A Ghostly Diversion
Secrets of Grasceby Manor
Return to De Grasceby Manor
James and the Air of Tragedy
The Haunting of Grasceby Rectory
Spectre of the Grasceby Flier
The Haunting of Lady Grasceby

All available as Kindle, print on demand and Kindle Unlimited from Amazon.

THE JAMES HANSONE GHOST MYSTERIES OMNIBUS VOL 1

The first five ghost mysteries all in one book.
Kindle, Paperback and Kindle Unlimited

Check out Paul's Amazon author page:
https://www.amazon.co.uk/Paul-L.-Money/e/
B003VNGE1M

THE FRAGILITY OF EXISTENCE

A Sci-Fi/Apocalyptic tale

The extermination of our species was probably inevitable when you look back with hindsight.

Every advanced civilisation has almost always wiped out the resident less advanced occupants whenever they came into contact. So it was the same for us, Homo Sapiens. But it wasn't supposed to have happened. We were not to know that.Perhaps that was a good thing. For the Universe ...

Matt and Simone stared out at the devastation and knew it could only mean one thing ...

Humanity was about to become extinct. Could they escape the fate they had seen befall others in their small village of 'Woldsfield'?They were not going to wait around to find out ...

Available on Amazon UK as Kindle or POD.

THE FRAGILITY OF SURVIVAL
A Sci-Fi/Apocalyptic tale
Book 2 of the Fragility series

Two couples on holiday in the Algarve
Two couples who like sunbathing on the beach
Two couples who like exploring the region
Scott and Katrina, Danny and Robyn

A simple two week holiday in the sun:
What could go wrong?
How about the end of the world as we know it for starters?
A desperate plight for one couple
an even more desperate plight for the other
as they discover the fragility of survival ...

Now available as Kindle, Paperback and Kindle Unlimited

THE STARVISTA 4 SAGA
Books 1 & 2 of a trilogy
Book 1: **The last Voyage of the StarVista 4**

A Voyage of a lifetime.
2700 passengers and crew.
The diary of an eight year old passenger.
Stunning encounters with fabulous interstellar destinations.
The mysterious multi inclined rings of the gas giant
planet Tianca in the hardly explored Cantrara system.

A 100 year mystery in the making...

Follow the adventures of Cherice Richmond on board the luxury star cruiser StarVista 4, with her parents, Carl and Natalie, the honourable newly appointed Earth Ambassadors to the Ziancan homeworld.
Little do they know that they will never return ...

THE FATE OF THE STARVISTA 4

The mystery of the Fate of the StarVista
4 unfolds in book 2 ...

In book 2 of the StarVista trilogy, 100 years after the disappearance of the passenger liner StarVista 4, Andrew James Hansone has been fascinated since a boy about what happened to the space liner. Having become highly successful and famous as a space ship designer with his own construction company, he resolves to solve the mystery once and for all.

But there is more to the disappearance of the
StarVista 4 than anyone realises ...

Join AJ as he sets out to fulfil his lifelong ambition
and discover The Fate of the StarVista 4.

Available on Amazon as Kindle, POD and Kindle Unlimited.

THAT SUMMER WE CHERISHED

"An Unlikely Friendship: A Summer Adventure in 1969"
As the summer of 1969 approached, Adam and Jocelyn had no idea that their paths would cross at Ashton Wood Farm in the Lincolnshire Wolds. Adam, a quiet and introverted nine year old, was dreading spending the summer at his aunt and uncle's farm.

Jocelyn, on the other hand, a twelve year old bursting with energy and curiosity, was eagerly looking forward to her time at her godparents' farm. Neither of them expected to see the other and their initial meeting did not go well.

For fans of "The Secret Garden" and "Bridge to Terabithia" and "Cider with Rosie," *That Summer We Cherished* is a heart-warming tale of two unlikely friends who find fun and adventure in each other's company. Don't miss out on this captivating story set in the summer of 1969.
Available on Amazon as Kindle, Paperback and Kindle Unlimited

ABOUT THE AUTHOR

Paul Money is an astronomy broadcaster, writer, public speaker and publisher. He was the Reviews Editor for the BBC Sky at Night magazine from 2006 until January 2024 before retiring from the role, and for eight years until 2013 he was one of three Astronomers on the Omega Holidays Northern Lights Flights.

He continues to give talks on astronomy and space as well as self publishing astronomy books and articles. Since 2016 he has written over a dozen novels, an omnibus of the first five ghost stories and two New Year Eve Tales volumes based on the characters found in the James Hansone Ghost Mysteries.

He is married to Lorraine whose hobby/interest is genealogy and family history and she is invaluable with her suggestions involving the historical aspects of all the novels.

As an astronomer Paul has been giving talks across the UK for over forty years and was awarded the Eric Zuker award for services to astronomy in 2002 by the Federation of Astronomical Societies. In October 2012 he was awarded the 'Sir Arthur Clarke Lifetime Achievement Award, 2012' for his 'tireless promotion of astronomy and space to the public'.

More info on the novels can be found at the Astrospace web site:
https://www.astrospace.co.uk/Fiction

January 2025

Printed in Great Britain
by Amazon

57191061R00066